TROUBLING LOVE

Elena Ferrante

TROUBLING LOVE

*Translated from the Italian
by Ann Goldstein*

Europa
editions

Europa Editions
27 Union Square West, Suite 302
New York, NY 10003
www.europaeditions.com
info@europaeditions.com

Copyright © 1999 by Edizioni e/o
First Publication 2006 by Europa Editions
Sixteenth printing, 2023

Translation by Ann Goldstein
Original title: *L'amore molesto*
Translation copyright © 2006 by Europa Editions

Library of Congress Cataloging in Publication Data is available
ISBN 978-1-933372-16-7

Ferrante, Elena
Troubling Love

Book design by Emanuele Ragnisco
www.mekkanografici.com

Printed in Italy

TROUBLING LOVE

For my mother

1.

My mother drowned on the night of May 23rd, my birthday, in the sea at a place called Spaccavento, a few miles from Minturno. In the late fifties, when my father was still living with us, we rented a room in a farmhouse in that very area and spent the month of July there, the five of us sleeping in a few burning-hot square meters. Every morning we girls drank a fresh egg, headed to the sea among tall reeds on paths of dirt and sand, and swam. The night my mother died, the owner of that house, who was called Rosa and by now was over seventy, had heard someone knocking at the door but, fearing thieves and murderers, didn't open it.

My mother had taken the train for Rome two days earlier, on May 21st, but had never arrived. Lately, she had been coming to stay with me at least once a month for a few days. I didn't like hearing her in the house. She woke at dawn and, as was her habit, cleaned the kitchen and living room from top to bottom. I tried to go back to sleep, but couldn't: rigid between the sheets, I had the impression that as she bustled about she transformed my body into that of a wizened child. When she came in with the coffee, I huddled to one side so that she wouldn't touch me as she sat down on the edge of the bed. Her sociability irritated me: she went shopping and got to know shopkeepers with whom in ten years I had exchanged no more than a word or two; she took walks through the city with casual acquaintances; she became a friend of my friends, and told them stories of her life, the same ones over and over. I, with her, could only be self-contained and insincere.

At the first hint of impatience on my part, she returned to

Naples. She gathered her things, gave a last tidying up to the house, and promised to be back soon. I went through the rooms rearranging according to my taste everything she had arranged according to hers. I put the saltshaker back on the shelf where I had kept it for years, I restored the detergent to the place that had always seemed to me convenient, I made a mess of the order she had brought to my drawers, I re-created chaos in the room where I worked. And in a little while the odor of her presence—a scent that left in the house a sense of restlessness—faded, like the smell of a passing shower in summer.

It often happened that she missed the train. Usually she arrived on the next one or even the next day, but I couldn't get used to it and so I worried just the same. I telephoned her anxiously. When I finally heard her voice, I reproached her with a certain harshness: why hadn't she departed, why hadn't she warned me? She apologized unremorsefully, wondering with amusement what I imagined could have happened to her, at her age. "Everything," I answered. I had always pictured a weft of traps, woven purposely to make her vanish from the world. When I was a child, I would spend the time of her absences waiting for her in the kitchen, at the window. I longed for her to appear at the end of the street like a figure in a crystal ball. I breathed on the glass, fogging it, in order not to see the street without her. If she was late, the anxiety became uncontainable, overflowing into tremors throughout my body. Then I ran to a storeroom, without windows or light, right next to her and my father's room. I closed the door and sat in the silent dark, crying. The little room was an effective antidote. It inspired a terror that kept at bay my anxiety for the fate of my mother. In the pitch-blackness, suffocating because of the smell of DDT, I was attacked by colored shapes that grazed the pupils of my eyes for a few seconds and left me gasping. "When you get back I'll kill you," I thought, as if it were she who had left me shut up in there. But then, as soon as I heard her voice in the hall, I quickly slipped out and went to hover near her, with an air of indifference. That storeroom came to my mind when I discovered that she had left at the normal time but had never arrived.

In the evening I got the first phone call. My mother said in a calm voice that she couldn't tell me anything: there was a man with her who was preventing her. Then she started laughing and hung up. At first what I mainly felt was bewilderment. I thought she was joking, and resigned myself to wait for a second phone call. In fact I spent hours in conjectures, sitting vainly beside the telephone. Finally, after midnight, I turned to a friend who was a policeman: he was very kind and told me not to get upset, he would take care of it. But the night passed without news of my mother. The only certainty was her departure: Signora De Riso, a widowed neighbor about the same age, with whom for fifteen years she had had alternating periods of friendliness and hostility, had told me on the telephone that she had gone with my mother to the station. While my mother stood in line to buy a ticket, the widow had bought her a bottle of water and a magazine. The train was crowded but my mother had found a place anyway, next to the window, in a compartment jammed with soldiers on leave. They had said goodbye, warning each other to be careful. How was she dressed? In the usual way, in clothes she had had for years: blue skirt and jacket, a black leather purse, old, low-heeled shoes, a worn suitcase.

At seven in the morning my mother telephoned again. Although I assailed her with questions ("Where are you? Where are you phoning from? Who are you with?"), she confined herself to reeling off, in a loud voice, a series of obscene expressions in dialect, uttering each one with enjoyment. Then she hung up. Those obscenities caused in me a disorienting regression. I telephoned my friend again, astonishing him with a confused mixture of Italian and expressions in dialect. He wanted to know if my mother had been particularly depressed recently. I didn't know. I admitted that she wasn't the way she used to be—calm, gently amused. She laughed for no reason, she talked too much; but old people often act like that. My friend agreed: as soon as the weather turned warm, old people were constantly doing odd things; there was nothing to worry about. But I continued to worry, and walked all over the city, searching in the places where I knew she liked to walk.

The third phone call came at ten at night. My mother spoke incoherently about a man who was following her so that he could take her away wrapped in a carpet. She asked me to come quickly and help her. I begged her to tell me where she was. She changed her tone, said that it was better not to. "Lock yourself in, don't open to anyone," she advised me. The man wanted to harm me, too. Then she added: "Go to sleep. I'm going to have a bath now." There was nothing more.

The next day two boys saw her body floating a few yards from the shore. She was wearing only her bra. Her suitcase wasn't found. Her blue suit wasn't found. Her underwear, her stockings, her shoes, her purse, with her papers, weren't found. But on her finger she still had her engagement ring and her wedding ring. In her ears were the earrings that my father had given her nearly half a century earlier.

I saw the body, and, faced with that livid object, felt that I had better grab onto it in order not to end up in some unknown place. It hadn't been assaulted. It showed only some bruises, a result of the waves that, though gentle, had pushed her all night against some rocks at the edge of the water. It seemed to me that around her eyes she had traces of heavy makeup. I observed for a long time, uneasily, her legs, olive-skinned, and extraordinarily youthful for a woman of sixty-three. With the same uneasiness I realized that the bra was very different from the shabby ones she usually wore. The cups were made of finely worked lace and revealed the nipples. They were joined by three embroidered "V"s, the signature of a Neapolitan shop that sold expensive lingerie for women, that of the Vossi sisters. When it was given to me, along with her earrings and her rings, I sniffed it for a long time. It had the sharp odor of new fabric.

2.

During the funeral I was surprised to find myself thinking that at last I no longer had any obligation to worry about her. Right afterward I was aware of a warm flow and felt wet between my legs.

I was at the head of a long procession of relatives, friends, acquaintances. My two sisters were close beside me. I was supporting one by the arm because I was afraid she might faint. The other was holding on to me as if her swollen eyes prevented her from seeing. That involuntary dissolving of my body frightened me like a threat of punishment. I had been unable to shed a tear: I couldn't cry, or maybe I hadn't wanted to cry. Furthermore, I was the only one who had expended any words of excuse for my father, who hadn't come to the funeral or sent flowers. My sisters hadn't concealed their disapproval, and now seemed intent on demonstrating publicly that they had enough tears to make up for those which neither I nor my father was shedding. I felt accused. When the procession was accompanied for a short stretch by a colored man who was carrying on his back some paintings mounted in frames, the first of which (the one visible on his back) showed a crude portrayal of a half-naked Gypsy, I hoped that neither they nor the relatives would notice. The maker of those paintings was my father. Maybe he was working on one of his trashy canvases at that very moment. He had made, for decades, and continued to make innumerable copies of that hateful Gypsy, sold on the streets and at country fairs, supplying for a few lire the constant demand of petit-bourgeois living rooms for ugly pictures. The irony of the lines that connect moments to meetings, to separations, to old rancors had sent to my mother's funeral not him but that elemental painting of his, detested by his daughters even more than we detested its author.

I felt tired of everything. I hadn't stopped for a moment since arriving in the city. For days I had been making the rounds with my Uncle Filippo, my mother's brother, through a chaos of offices, visiting small-time brokers who might be able to speed the bureaucratic procedures, or, after waiting in long lines at windows, testing the willingness of clerks to overcome insurmountable obstacles in exchange for generous gratuities. At times my uncle succeeded in obtaining results by showing the empty sleeve of his jacket. He had lost his right arm at an advanced age, fifty-six, working at a lathe in a workshop on the outskirts of the city, and, ever since, he had used his disability to ask favors, or to wish the same bad luck on those who refused him. But we got the best results by handing out a lot of undeserved money. By that means we had procured the necessary documents, permissions from I don't know how many proper authorities, true or invented, a first-class funeral, and, hardest of all, a place in the cemetery.

Meanwhile the dead body of Amalia, my mother, butchered by the autopsy, had grown heavier and heavier as we dragged it, along with name and surname, date of birth and date of death, before bureaucrats who were sometimes rude, sometimes ingratiating. I felt the urgency of getting rid of it and yet, still not sufficiently exhausted, I wanted to help carry the casket. They had given in to me after a lot of resistance: women do not carry caskets. It had been a terrible idea. Since the men who were carrying the casket with me (a cousin and my two brothers-in-law) were taller, I was afraid during the entire journey that the wooden box might slide into me, between the collarbone and the neck, along with the body it contained. When the coffin was set down in the hearse, and it had started off, a few steps and a guilty relief were enough for the tension to release that hidden stream from my womb.

The warm liquid that was coming out of me against my will gave me the impression of an agreed-upon signal among aliens inside my body. The funeral procession advanced toward Piazza Carlo III. The yellowish façade of the Reclusorio seemed barely able to contain the pressure of the Incis neighborhood that weighed on it. The streets of topographic memory seemed to me unstable, like a carbonated drink that, if shaken, bubbles up and overflows. I felt the city coming apart in the heat, in the dusty gray light, and I went over in my mind the story of childhood and adolescence that impelled me to wander along the Veterinaria to the Botanic Gardens, or over the cobbles of the market of Sant'Antonio Abate, which were always damp and strewn with rotting vegetables. I had the impression that my mother was carrying off the places, too, and the names of the streets. I stared at the image of my sisters and me in the glass, among the wreaths of flowers, like a photograph taken in dim light, useless for future memory. I anchored myself to the paving stones of the piazza with the soles of my shoes, I isolated the scent of the flowers arranged on the hearse, which was already putrid. At a certain point I was afraid that the blood would start running down my ankles, and I tried to get free of my sisters. It was impossible. I had to wait until the procession wound through the piazza, ascended via Don Bosco, and broke up in a crush of cars and people. Aunts and uncles, great-aunts and uncles, in-laws, cousins began to embrace us in turn: people vaguely known, changed by the years, seen only in childhood or perhaps never. The few people I recalled clearly hadn't shown up. Or maybe they were there, but I didn't recognize them because I could recall only details from my childhood: a crossed eye, a lame leg, the olive color of the skin. To make up for it, people whose names I didn't even know drew me aside to recite old wrongs done to them by my father. Unknown but affectionate young men, adept at social conversation, asked me how I was, how things were going, what kind of work I did. I answered: well, it was going well, I drew comic strips, and how were things going for them? Many wrinkled old women, completely in black except for the pallor of their faces, praised the extraordinary beauty and goodness of Amalia. Some embraced me with such force and shed such copious tears that I wavered between a feeling of suffocation and an unbearable sensation of wetness that extended from their sweat and tears to my groin, to where my thighs joined. For the first time I was glad about the dark dress I was wearing. I was about to leave when Uncle Filippo went off on one of his rants. In his seventy-year-old head, which often confused past and present, a detail must have knocked down barriers that were already shaky. To everyone's astonishment, he began cursing loudly in dialect, and frantically waving the only arm he had.

"Did you see Caserta?" he asked, turning to me and my sisters, barely able to breathe. And again and again he repeated that well-known name, a threatening sound from childhood that made me apprehensive. Then, turning livid, he added, "No shame. At Amalia's funeral. If your father had been there, he would have murdered him."

I didn't want to hear about Caserta, a pure agglomerate of childhood fear. I pretended it was nothing and tried to calm him down, but he didn't even hear me. Rather, in his agitation he squeezed me with his one arm, as if he wished to console me for the insult of that name. So I pulled myself away rudely, promised my sisters that I would get to the cemetery in time for the burial ceremony, and returned to the piazza. Quickly I looked for a bar. I asked for the bathroom and went toward the back, into a tiny stinking room with a dirty toilet and a yellow-stained sink.

The flow of blood was heavy. I felt nauseous and slightly dizzy. In the shadows I saw my mother, her legs spread, as she unhooked a safety pin and, as if they were pasted on, removed some bloody linen rags from her sex; without surprise she turned and said to me, calmly, "Go on, what are you doing here?" I burst into tears for the first time in many years. I wept, banging one hand at almost regular intervals on the sink, as if to impose a rhythm on my tears. When I realized it, I stopped, cleaned myself as well as I could with some Kleenex, and went out in search of a drugstore.

It was then that I saw him for the first time. "May I be of help?" he asked when I bumped into him: an instant, time to feel against my face the material of his shirt, notice the blue cap of the pen that stuck out of his jacket pocket, and meanwhile register the uncertain tone of voice, a pleasant odor, the sagging skin of his neck, a thick mass of white hair, neatly combed.

"Do you know where there's a drugstore?" I asked without even looking at him, engaged as I was in a rapid swerve intended to cancel out that contact.

"On Corso Garibaldi," he answered as I re-established a minimum of distance between the compact smear of his bony body and me. Now, in his white shirt and dark jacket, he was as if pasted to the façade of the Albergo dei Poveri. I saw him pale, carefully shaved, without wonder in a gaze that I disliked. I thanked him almost in a whisper, and went in the direction he had indicated.

He followed me with his voice, which changed from courteous to a threatening hiss of words that became more and more vulgar. I was hit by a stream of obscenities in dialect, a soft river of sound that involved me, my sisters, my mother in a concoction of semen, saliva, feces, urine, in every possible orifice.

I turned suddenly, all the more astonished as the insults were unmotivated. But the man was no longer there. Maybe he had crossed the street and disappeared among the cars, maybe he had turned the corner toward Sant'Antonio Abate. Slowly I let the pounding of my heart become normal and an ugly homicidal impulse evaporate. I went into the drugstore, bought a package of tampons, and went back to the bar.

3.

I arrived at the cemetery in a taxi, just in time to see the coffin lowered into a pit of gray stone, which was then filled with earth. My sisters left right after the burial, by car, with their husbands and their children. They couldn't wait to get home and forget. We embraced and promised to see each other again soon, but we knew that we wouldn't. At most we would, from time to time, exchange phone calls, to measure the increasing rate of mutual estrangement. For years we had all three lived in different cities, each with our own life and a past in common that we didn't like. The rare times we met we preferred to be silent about all the things we had to say to each other.

Left alone, I thought that Uncle Filippo would invite me to his house, where I had been staying for the past few days. But he didn't. I had announced to him in the morning that I had to go to my mother's apartment, to pick up the few objects that had sentimental value, and cancel the lease, the electricity, the gas, the telephone; and he had probably thought it was pointless to ask me. He went off without saying goodbye, bent, with dragging feet, worn out by age and by that sudden accumulation of old rancors that made him vomit up extravagant insults.

So I was forgotten on the street. The crowd of relatives departed to the outlying neighborhoods from which they had come. My mother had been buried by insolent undertakers at the bottom of a pit stinking of wax and decaying flowers. I had a backache and stomach cramps. I made up my mind reluctantly: I walked along the burning-hot wall of the Botanic Garden to Piazza Cavour, in air made heavier by the exhaust from the cars and the buzz of dialect sounds that I deciphered unwillingly.

It was the language of my mother, which I had vainly tried to forget, along with many other things about her. When we saw each other at my house, or I came to Naples for fleeting, half-day visits, she would make an effort to use a stiff Italian, and, in annoyance, just to help her, I would slip into dialect. Not a joyous or nostalgic dialect but unnatural, used inexpertly, pronounced stiltedly, like a barely known foreign language. In the sounds that I uttered uneasily was an echo of the violent quarrels between Amalia and my father, between my father and her relatives, between her and the relatives of my father. I became impatient. Soon I returned to my Italian and she settled into her dialect. Now that she was dead and I could eliminate it forever, along with the memory that it conveyed, hearing it provoked anxiety. I used that language to buy a *pizza fritta* stuffed with ricotta. After days of near-fasting, I ate with pleasure, wandering through the neglected gardens with their struggling oleanders, and scanning the many groups of old people. The assaultive traffic of people and cars near the gardens made me decide to go to my mother's.

Amalia's apartment was on the fourth floor of an old building girded with scaffolding. The building was one of those edifices in the city center that were half deserted at night and during the day inhabited by clerks who renew licenses, hunt down birth or residency certificates, interrogate computers for reservations or tickets on planes, trains, and ships, draft insurance policies for theft, fire, illness, death, compile complicated statements of income. The ordinary tenants were few, but when my father, more than twenty years earlier—the moment

Amalia told him that she wanted to separate from him, and we daughters firmly supported her in that choice—chased all four of us out of the house, it was there that, by chance, we had found an apartment to rent. I had never liked the building. It made me restless, like a prison, a court, a hospital. My mother, however, liked it: she found it imposing. In fact it was ugly and dirty, right down to the big outside door, which was routinely forced open every time the superintendent had the lock repaired. The panels were dusty, blackened by exhaust fumes, with big brass knobs that hadn't been polished since the start of the century. During the day, there was always someone standing in the long cavernous passage that led to an internal courtyard: students, people waiting for the bus that stopped a little farther on, peddlers selling lighters, Kleenex, toasted corn or roasted chestnuts, tourists sheltering from the heat or the rain, surly men of all races in perennial contemplation of the display windows that ran along the two walls. Usually these men passed the time waiting for whatever staring at the art photographs of an elderly photographer who had a studio in the building: brides and bridegrooms in their wedding outfits, smiling, luminous girls, youths in uniform with impudent expressions. Years earlier a passport-type photograph of Amalia had also been displayed for a couple of days. I myself had warned the photographer to remove it, before my father, passing by, flew into a rage and smashed the window.

I crossed the inner courtyard with my eyes lowered and went up the short flight of steps that led to the glass door of stairway B. The porter was absent and I was relieved. I got into the elevator quickly. It was the only place in that whole building that I liked. In general I wasn't fond of those metal sarcophagi that rise rapidly or plunge down as soon as you touch the button, making a pit in your stomach. But this one had wood-paneled walls, glass doors with gray arabesques around the edges and fine brass handles, two graceful wooden benches that faced each other, a mirror, and dim lighting; and it lurched up and down with a concert of squeaks, at a restful pace. A coin box from the fifties, with a broad belly and a curved beak pointing upward, ready to swallow change, emitted a metallic sigh at every floor. Although for many years now the car had been set in motion by the mere press of a button, the coin box remained uselessly nailed to the right-hand wall. Yet, while it disrupted the tranquil old age of that space, the box, with its abstinent emptiness, didn't displease me.

I sat on a bench and did what, as a girl, I had done whenever I needed to calm myself: instead of pressing the button with the number 4 on it, I let myself go up to the sixth floor. That space had been empty and dark for many years, ever since the lawyer who had his office there had left, taking with him even the light bulb from the landing. When the elevator stopped, I let my breath glide into my stomach and then return slowly to my throat. As always, after a few seconds, the light in the elevator went out, too. I thought of reaching my hand out to one of the door handles: you had only to pull it and the light would return. But I didn't move and continued to send my breath deep into my body. The only sound was that of the woodworms eating into the paneled walls.

Just a few months earlier (five, six?), on a sudden impulse, I had revealed to my mother, during one of my brief visits, that as an adolescent I used to retreat to that secret place, and I brought her up there, to the top. Maybe I wanted to try to establish an intimacy that there had never been, maybe I wanted to let her know in some confused way that I had always been unhappy. But she seemed to me only amused by the fact that I had sat suspended in the void, in a dilapidated elevator.

"Have you ever, in all these years, had a man?" I had then asked her, point-blank. I meant had she ever had a lover, after leaving my father? It was an anomalous question, among the possible questions between us since I was a child. But her body, seated a few inches from mine on the wooden bench, had manifested no unease. Not even her voice, which had been sure and clear: no. Not a single sign that might lead me to think that she was lying. Thus I had no doubt. She was lying.

"You have a lover," I said to her coldly.

Her reaction had been exaggerated compared with her normal self-restraint. She had pulled her dress up to her waist, revealing baggy waist-high pink underpants. Giggling, she had said something confused about her soft flesh, her sagging belly, repeating, "Touch here," and tried to take one of my hands to place it on her flabby white stomach.

I had pulled back and rested my hand on my heart to calm its rapid beating. She let fall the hem of her dress, but her knees were still uncovered, yellow in the light of the elevator. I regretted having brought her to my refuge. Above all I wanted her to cover herself. "Get out," I had said to her. She had in fact done so: she never said no to me. A single step beyond the open doors and she had disappeared into darkness. Alone in the car, I had felt a peaceful pleasure. With an unreflecting gesture I had closed the doors. After a few seconds the light in the elevator went out.

"Delia," my mother had murmured, but without alarm. She never showed alarm in my presence, and even on that occasion it had seemed to me that, out of long habit, instead of looking for reassurance, she intended to reassure me.

I had sat for a while tasting my name like an echo of memory, an abstraction that sounds without sound in one's head. It seemed to me the voice, from time immemorial, of when she searched for me in the house and couldn't find me.

Now I was there and trying to quickly cancel out the memory of that echo. But I still had the impression of not being alone. I was being spied on, not by that Amalia of months before who now was dead but by me coming out on the landing to see myself sitting there. I hated myself, when that happened. I was ashamed to discover myself mute in the obsolete car, suspended between void and darkness, hidden as if in a nest on the branch of a tree, with the long tail of the steel cables dangling wearily from the body of the elevator. I stretched out my hand toward the door and groped for the handle. The darkness withdrew beyond the arabesqued glass.

I had always known it. There was a line that I couldn't cross when I thought of Amalia. Perhaps I was there in order to cross it. That frightened me. I pressed the button with the number 4 and the elevator jolted noisily. Creaking, it began to descend toward my mother's apartment.

4.

I asked for the keys from the neighbor, the widow De Riso. She gave them to me but refused definitively to go in with me. She was fat and suspicious, and had a big mole on her right cheek that was inhabited by two long gray whiskers. Her hair was parted in the middle and gathered at the back in a twist of braids. She was dressed in black: perhaps it was habitual, perhaps because she was still wearing her dress from the funeral. She stood on the threshold of her apartment and watched me choose the right keys. But the door hadn't been carefully locked. Contrary to her usual habit, Amalia had used only one of the two locks, the one that took two turns of the key. The other, which took five, she hadn't used.

"What's happened?" I asked the neighbor, pushing open the door.

De Riso hesitated. "Her head was a little in the clouds," she said, but she must have considered the expression disrespectful, because she added, "She was happy." Then she hesitated again: it was clear that she would willingly have gossiped but she feared the ghost of my mother hovering over the stairwell, in the apartment, and certainly in her house as well. I invited her again to enter, hoping that she would keep me company with her chatter. She refused firmly, with a shudder, and her eyes filled with tears.

"Why was she happy?" I asked.

She hesitated again and then made up her mind.

"For some time a man had been coming to see her, a tall man, very respectable . . . "

I gave her a hostile glance. I decided that I didn't want her to continue.

"He was her brother," I said.

Signora De Riso narrowed her eyes, insulted: she and my mother had been friends for a long time and she knew perfectly well who Uncle Filippo was. He was neither tall nor very respectable.

"Her brother," she pronounced with false compliance.

"No?" I asked, annoyed by her tone. She said goodbye to me coldly and closed the door.

When one enters the house of a person who has just died, it's hard to believe that it's deserted. Houses don't have ghosts, but they contain the effects of life's final gestures. First I heard the rush of water from the kitchen and for a fraction of a second, with an abrupt torsion of the true and the false, I thought that my mother wasn't dead, that her death had been merely the subject of a long, painful fantasy that had begun in some long-ago time. I was sure that she was in the house, alive, standing at the sink, washing the dishes and murmuring to herself. But the shutters were closed, the apartment was dark. I turned on the light and saw that the water was streaming copiously into the empty sink from the old brass tap.

I turned it off. My mother belonged to a fading culture that could not conceive of waste. She wouldn't throw away stale bread, she used the rind of the cheese, putting it in the soup to flavor it, she almost never bought meat but at the butcher

asked for scrap bones to make broth, and then sucked on them
as if they contained a miraculous substance. She would never
have forgotten the tap. She used water with a frugality that was
transformed into a reflex of gesture, ear, voice. If as a girl I left
even a silent thread of water, extending to the bottom of the
sink like a knitting needle, she would call to me an instant later,
without reproach, "Delia, the tap." I felt uneasy: she had wasted more water with that distraction in the last hours of life than
in all her existence. I saw her floating face down, suspended in
the middle of the kitchen, against the background of blue
majolica tiles.

I moved on in a hurry. I went through the bedroom, throw-
ing the few things she had cared about in a plastic bag: the
album of family photographs, a bracelet, an old winter dress of
hers from the fifties that I liked, too. The rest not even the
junkmen would have wanted. The few pieces of furniture were
old and ugly, her bed was only a mattress and box spring, the
sheets and blankets had been mended with a care that, given
their age, they didn't deserve. It struck me, though, that the
drawer where she usually kept her underwear was empty. I
looked for the laundry bag and peered inside. There was nothing but a man's shirt, of a good quality.

I examined it. It was a blue shirt, medium-sized, bought
recently and chosen by a young man or a man of youthful
tastes. The collar was dirty but the odor of the fabric was not
unpleasant: the sweat was fused with an expensive brand of
deodorant. I folded it carefully and put it in the plastic bag
along with the other things. It was not a garment that Uncle
Filippo would have worn.

I then went into the bathroom. There was neither tooth-
brush nor toothpaste. Her old blue bathrobe was hanging on
the door. The toilet paper was nearly finished. Beside the toilet there was a half-full garbage bag. There was no garbage
inside: instead there was the stink of a tired body preserved by

clothes that are dirty or made of an old fabric, every fiber saturated with the humors of decades. I began to take out, piece by piece, with a slight disgust, all my mother's intimate garments: pink and white underpants, much mended and with ancient elastic that showed here and there through the torn seams, like train tracks in the gap between one tunnel and the next; shapeless, threadbare bras; undershirts full of holes; garters of the sort that were used forty years ago and that she had kept for no reason; panty hose in a sorry state; faded slips, with yellowed lace, that had been out of fashion and obsolete for a long time.

Amalia, who had always dressed shabbily because she was poor but also because she was in the habit of not making herself attractive—a habit acquired many decades earlier to placate the jealousy of my father—seemed to have suddenly decided to get rid of her entire wardrobe. I remembered the only garment she had been wearing when they fished her out: the elegant brand-new bra, with the three "V"s that joined the cups. The image of her breasts wrapped in that lace increased my unease. I left the garments scattered on the floor, without the strength to touch them again; I closed the door and leaned against it.

But to no purpose: the entire bathroom jumped over me and recomposed itself in front of me, in the hall: Amalia now was sitting on the toilet and watching me closely while I removed the hair from my legs. I coated my ankles with hot wax and then, groaning, pulled it away from the skin, with a decisive gesture. She, meanwhile, was telling me that as a girl she had cut the black hair off her ankles with scissors. But it had grown back immediately, stiff as coils of barbed wire. At the beach, too, before putting on her bathing suit, she shortened her pubic hairs with scissors.

I put the waxing cream on her, although she tried to shield herself. I spread the wax carefully on her ankles, on the inside of her firm thin thighs, her groin, reproaching her meanwhile with unreasonable harshness for her mended slip. Then I peeled off the wax while she observed me impassively. I did it carelessly, as if I wanted to subject her to a painful trial, and she let me, without saying a word, as if she had agreed to the trial. But her skin didn't resist. It turned fiery red and then immediately purple, revealing a network of broken capillaries. "It doesn't matter," she said, "it will pass," while I weakly reproached myself for what I'd done to her.

I reproached myself more intensely now, as with an effort of will I tried to send the bathroom back behind the door I was leaning against. To manage it, I moved away from the door, let the image of her purple legs fade into the hall, and went to the kitchen to get my purse. When I returned to the bathroom, I looked carefully among the underpants that were lying on the floor and chose the pair that seemed to me the least worn. I washed, and changed my tampax. I left my underpants on the floor, among Amalia's. As I passed the mirror I smiled involuntarily, to calm myself.

I don't know how long I sat beside the kitchen window, listening to the din in the alley, the traffic of motorbikes, the tramp of feet on the pavement. The street gave off an odor of stagnant water that rose through the scaffolding. I was exhausted but didn't want to lie down on Amalia's bed or ask Uncle Filippo for help or telephone my father or look again for Signora De Riso. I felt pity for that world of lost old people: confused by images of themselves that went back to bygone eras, they were sometimes in harmony, sometimes at odds with the shades of things and people of the past. Yet I had trouble keeping myself on the margins. I was tempted to link voice to voice, thing to thing, fact to fact. Already now I felt Amalia return, wanting to observe how I rubbed creams into my skin, how I put on my makeup and took it off. Already I began to imagine resentfully a secret old age in which she played with her body all day, as perhaps she would have done as a young woman if my father had not read in such games a desire to please others, a preparation for infidelity.

5.

I slept no more than a couple of hours, without dreams. When I opened my eyes, the room was dark and from the open window came only the nebulous glow of the streetlamps, diffused over a segment of the ceiling. Amalia was up there like a nocturnal butterfly, young, perhaps twenty, wrapped in a green bathrobe, her stomach swelled by advanced pregnancy. She lay on her back, and although her face was serene, her body, caught in a painful spasm, twisted convulsively. I closed my eyes to give her time to detach herself from the ceiling and return to death; then I reopened them and looked at the clock. It was two-thirty. I slept again but only for a few minutes. Then I fell into a torpor crowded with images, in which, without wanting to, I began to tell myself about my mother.

Amalia, in my waking sleep, was an olive-skinned, hairy woman. Her hair, even when she was old, even when it was faded by the salt air, gleamed like the skin of a panther, and it was thick, so thick that no wind could penetrate. It smelled of laundry soap, but not the dry kind, with a ladder printed on the package. It smelled of a brown liquid soap that was bought in a basement: I remembered the tickle of dust in my nostrils and throat.

The soap was sold by a fat, hairless man. He scooped it up with a trowel and stuck it on thick yellow paper, depositing with it a stench of sweat and DDT. I ran to Amalia breathlessly, holding the package and, with puffed cheeks, blowing on it, to get rid of the odors of the basement and of that man; I'm running the same way now, even though so much time has passed, with my cheek on my mother's pillow. And she, seeing me arrive, is already loosening her hair, and it comes undone as if she had sculpted it in spirals above her forehead and the blackness of the hairdo were changing molecular structure under her hands.

Her hair was long. Amalia was always undoing it, and washing it took not just soap but the entire container of the man in the cellar at the foot of steps that were white with ashes or lye. I suspected that at times my mother, escaping my surveillance, went and dipped her hair straight into the barrel, with the consent of the man in the shop. Then she would turn toward me gaily with her face wet, the water streaming down her neck from the tap in our kitchen, eyelashes and pupils black, eyebrows drawn with charcoal, lightly whitened by the suds that, arching over her forehead, fragmented into drops of soap and water. The drops slid down over her nose, toward her mouth, until she caught them with her red tongue, and it seemed to me that she was saying: "Good."

I didn't know how she managed to be in two different spaces at the same time, in the soap barrel in the cellar, in her blue slip, the straps falling off her shoulders and down her arms; and meanwhile abandoning herself to the water in our kitchen, which was giving her hair a liquid sheen. Certainly I had dreamed it that way countless times with my eyes open, as I did now yet again, and yet again felt a painful embarrassment.

The fat man in fact was not content with standing and watching. In summer he dragged the barrel outside. He was bare-chested, bronzed by the sun, and wore a white handkerchief tied tight around his forehead. He poked around in the container with a long stick and, sweating, twisted the shining mass of Amalia's hair. Meanwhile, down the street, a steamroller crackled, advancing slowly with its big cylinder of gray stone. Another man drove it, thickset and muscular, also bare-chested, the hair in his armpits curly with sweat. He wore a type of khaki trousers unbuttoned in such a way as to show, at the level of his stomach, a frightening hollow, and, settled on the seat of the machine, he surveyed the dense and shiny tar of Amalia's hair as it slid out from the tilted drum and extended over the crushed stone, steaming, and rippling the air. My mother's hair was pitch and it spread out into a luxuriant down that thickened in the prohibited places of the body. Prohibited to me: she wouldn't let me touch her. She hid her face, tossing the curtain of hair over it, and offered her neck to the sun to dry.

When the telephone rang, she pulled her head up suddenly, so that the wet hair flew from the floor through the air, grazing the ceiling and falling on her back with a slap that woke me completely. I turned on the light. I couldn't remember where the telephone was, and meanwhile it kept ringing. I found it in the hall, an old telephone of the sixties that I knew well, attached to the wall. When I answered a male voice called me Amalia.

"I'm not Amalia," I said. "Who is it?"

I had the impression that the man on the telephone struggled to repress a laugh. He repeated, "I'm not Amalia," in falsetto, and then resumed, in the purest dialect: "Leave the bag with the dirty clothes on the top floor. You promised it to me. And look carefully: you'll find the suitcase with your things. I put it there for you."

"Amalia is dead," I said in a calm voice. "Who are you?"

"Caserta," said the man.

The name sounded like the name of the bogeyman in a fable.

"I'm Delia," I answered. "What is on the top floor? What do you have of hers?"

"I, nothing. It's you who have something of mine," the man said, again in falsetto, distorting my Italian in an affected manner.

"You come here," I said to him in a persuasive tone. "We can talk about it and you can take what you need."

There was a long silence. I waited for an answer but there was none. The man had not hung up: he had simply let go of the receiver and walked away.

I went to the kitchen and drank a glass of water; the water was dense and had a terrible smell. Then I returned to the telephone and dialed Uncle Filippo's number. He answered after five rings and before I could even say hello, began shouting into the telephone insults of every sort.

"It's Delia," I said harshly. I felt that he was having trouble identifying me. When he remembered me, he began to mutter excuses, calling me "my child," and asking again and again if I was all right, where I was, what had happened.

"Caserta called me," I said. Then, before he could start again on the rosary of curses, I ordered him, "Calm down."

6.

Afterward I went back to the bathroom. With one foot I kicked my dirty underpants behind the bidet, and then picked up Amalia's lingerie, which I had scattered over the floor, and put it back in the garbage bag. Then I went out to the landing. I was no longer either depressed or uneasy. I carefully closed the door, using both locks, and pushed the button for the elevator.

Once inside, I pressed the button for the sixth floor. At the top, I left the doors of the elevator open so that the dark space was at least partly illuminated. I discovered that the man had lied: my mother's suitcase wasn't there. I thought of going back down but changed my mind. I placed the garbage bag in the rectangle of light left by the elevator and then closed the doors. In the dark I settled myself in a corner of the landing from which I could see clearly anyone who came out of the elevator or arrived by the stairs. I sat on the floor.

For decades, Caserta had been for me a city of haste, a restless place where everything went faster than in other places. Not the royal city to whose eighteenth-century park with its cascading waterfalls I had gone as a child the Monday after Easter, and where, amid hordes of day-trippers, lost in a vast clan of relatives, I ate salami from Secondigliano and hardboiled eggs inside an oily, peppery dough. Of the city and the park memory could put into words only the rapid streams of water and the terrifying pleasure of getting lost as the shouts calling me back grew more and more distant. But what my less easily verbalized emotions recorded under the word Caserta was a spinning nausea, vertigo, and a lack of air. Sometimes that place, which belonged to a less reliable memory, consisted of a dimly lighted staircase and a wrought-iron banister. At other times it was a patch of light striped by bars and covered by a fine screen, which I observed crouching underground, in the company of a child named Antonio, who held me tightly by the hand. The sounds that accompanied it, like the soundtrack of a film, were pure commotion, sudden banging, as of things formerly in order that abruptly collapse. The odor was of lunchtime or dinnertime, when, coming from every doorway, the smells of the various dishes mingle in the stairwell but are ruined by a stink of mold and cobwebs. Caserta was a place where I wasn't supposed to go, a bar with a sign: a dark woman, palm trees, lions, camels. It had the taste of sugared almonds in an exquisite candy box, but you were forbidden to enter. If little girls went in they never came out again. Not even my mother was supposed to go there, or my father would kill her. Caserta was a man, a silhouette of dark fabric. The silhouette, hanging on a thread, rotated, turning first one way, then the other. We were not allowed to mention him. Amalia was often chased through the house, caught, struck in the face first with the back of the hand, then the palm, only because she had said: "Caserta."

This in my less datable memories. In the clearer ones there was Amalia herself who spoke of him secretly, of that man-city of waterfalls and hedges and stone statues and pictures of palm trees and camels. She didn't speak of him to me, who perhaps was playing under the table with my sisters. She spoke of him to others, to the women who were making gloves with her at home. Somewhere in my brain I preserved echoes of phrases. One remained very clear in my mind. It was not even words, or no longer was, but sounds compacted and made concrete in an image. That Caserta, my mother said in a whisper, had pushed her into a corner and tried to kiss her. I, hearing her, saw the man's open mouth, with bright white teeth and a long red tongue. The tongue shot out from the lips and retracted at a velocity that hypnotized me. As an adolescent I would close my eyes on purpose to reproduce that scene, and would contemplate it with a mixture of attraction and repulsion. But I felt guilty, as if I were doing something forbidden. By then I knew that in that image of fantasy there was a secret that could not be revealed, not because one part of me didn't know how to get to it but because, if I did, the other part would have refused to name it and would have driven me out.

On the telephone, just before, Uncle Filippo had said to me some things that I already knew in a confused way: he spoke of them and I knew. They could be summed up thus: Caserta was a contemptible man. As a boy he had been a friend of his and of my father. After the war, they had had some profitable business dealings: he had seemed a clear-headed, sincere young man. But he had eyed my mother. And not only her: he was already married, he had a son, but he bothered all the women in the neighborhood. When he went too far, my uncle and my father had taught him a lesson. And Caserta with his wife and child had gone to live in another place. My uncle had concluded in a threatening dialect: "He wouldn't get her out of his head. So we made the desire get out forever."

Silence. I had seen blood between cries and insults. Ghosts upon ghosts. Antonio, the child who held my hand, had gone down into the darkest part of the basement. For an instant I felt the domestic violence of my childhood and adolescence return to my eyes and ears as if it were oozing along a thread that joined us. But I realized for the first time that now, after so many years, it was what I wanted.

"I'm coming over," Uncle Filippo had suggested.

"What do you think a man of seventy can do to me?"

He was confused. Before hanging up I had promised that I would call him back if I heard from Caserta again.

Now I was waiting on the landing. At least an hour passed. The glow of lights in the stairwell from the other floors allowed me to check, once I got used to the dark, the whole area. Nothing happened. Finally around four in the morning the elevator jerked abruptly and the light went from green to red. The car slid down.

With a leap I was at the railing: I saw it glide past the fifth floor and stop at the fourth. The doors opened and closed. Then silence again. Even the echo of the vibrations emitted by the steel cables disappeared.

I waited a little, maybe five minutes; then I went cautiously down one flight. There was a dim yellow light: the three doors that faced the landing led to the offices of an insurance company. I went down another flight, slipping around the dark, still elevator car. I wanted to look inside but I didn't, taken by surprise: the door of my mother's house was wide open, the lights were on. Right on the threshold was Amalia's suitcase and beside it her black leather purse. I was about to rush instinctively toward those objects when behind me I heard the click of the elevator's glass doors. The light illumined the car, revealing an old man, well groomed, his dark, fleshless face handsome in its way beneath a mass of white hair. He was sitting on one of the wooden benches and was so still that he seemed like an enlargement of an old photograph. He stared at me for a second with a friendly, slightly melancholy look. Then the car rose upward with a rumble.

I had no doubts. The man was the same one who had reeled off the litany of obscenities during Amalia's funeral. But I hesitated to follow him up the stairs: I thought I should but I felt as if attached to the floor, like a statue. I stared at the elevator cables until the car stopped with a clatter of the doors as they rapidly opened and closed. A few seconds later the car slid past me again. Before it disappeared toward the ground floor the man showed me, with a smile, the garbage bag that contained my mother's underwear.

7.

I was strong, lean, quick, and decisive; not only that, I liked being confident of being so. But I don't know what happened in that situation. Maybe it was exhaustion, maybe it was the shock of finding open that door that I had diligently closed. Maybe I was dazed by the house with the lights on, by my mother's suitcase and purse in full view in the doorway. Or maybe it was something else. It was the repulsion I felt at perceiving that the image of that old man beyond the arabesqued glass of the elevator had seemed for a moment to have a dark beauty. So, instead of following him, I stood motionless, trying to fix in my mind the details, even after the elevator disappeared into the stairwell.

When I came to myself, I felt drained, depressed by the sensation of being humiliated in front of the part of myself that watched over every possible yielding of the other. I went to the window in time to see the man going off along the alley in the light of the streetlamps, his body erect, at a slow but not labored pace, the bag in his right hand with the arm held stiffly down, the black plastic grazing the pavement. I went back to the door and was about to rush down the stairs. But I realized that the neighbor, Signora De Riso, had appeared in a vertical strip of light cautiously opening between the door and the frame.

She was wearing a long pink cotton nightgown, and she was looking at me with hostility, her face split by the chain that was meant to keep anyone with evil intentions from entering. Certainly she had been there for some time, spying through the peephole and listening.

"What's going on?" she asked argumentatively. "You've been up and down all night." I was about to answer in an equally argumentative tone, but I remembered that she had mentioned a man my mother was seeing and was in time to realize that I had better control myself, if I wanted to know more. I was now obliged to hope that that hint of gossip which had annoyed me in the afternoon would become detailed talk, conversation, compensation for that lonely old woman who didn't know how to get through her nights.

"Nothing," I said, trying to make my breathing normal. "I can't sleep."

She muttered something about how the dead have trouble leaving.

"The first night, they never let you sleep," she said.

"Did you hear any noise? Did I disturb you?" I asked with false politeness.

"I sleep little and not very well, after a certain time. On top of that there was the lock: you kept opening and closing the door."

"It's true," I said. "I'm a little nervous. I dreamed that that man you were telling me about was here on the landing."

The old woman understood that I had changed my tune and was disposed to listen to her gossip, but she wanted to be sure that I wouldn't reject her again.

"What man?" she asked.

"The one you told me about . . . the one who came here, to visit my mother. I fell asleep thinking about him . . . "

"He was a respectable man, who put Amalia in a good mood. He brought her *sfogliatelle* and flowers. When he came, I heard them talking and laughing continuously. She, especially, laughed—her laugh was so loud you could hear it from the landing."

"What were they saying?"

"I don't know, I wouldn't stay and listen. I mind my own business."

I made a gesture of impatience.

"But Amalia never talked about him?"

"Yes," Signora De Riso admitted. "Once I saw them come out of the house together. She told me that he was someone she had known for fifty years, who was almost like a relative. And if that's so, you know him, too. He was tall, thin, with white hair. Your mother treated him almost as if he were her brother. As an intimate."

"What was his name?"

"I don't know. She never told me. Amalia did as she liked. One day she told me about all her affairs, even if I didn't want to hear it, and the next day she didn't even say hello. I know about the *sfogliatelle* because they didn't eat them all and she gave the rest to me. She also gave me the flowers, because the scent gave her a headache: she always had a headache, in recent months. But invite me in and introduce me, never."

"Maybe she was afraid of embarrassing you."

"No, she wanted to mind her own business. I understood and stayed away. But I want to tell you that your mother was not to be trusted."

"In what sense?"

"She didn't behave properly. This man I met only the one time. He was a handsome old man, well dressed, and when I met them he made me a slight bow. She, however, turned the other way and said an ugly word to me."

"Maybe you misunderstood."

"I understood very well. She had developed a mania for saying the worst words, out loud, even when she was alone. And then she would start laughing. I heard her from here, in my kitchen."

"My mother never said bad words."

"She did, she did . . . At a certain age, one should have some restraint."

"It's true," I said. And there returned to my mind the suitcase and purse in the doorway of the apartment. They seemed to me objects that, because of the journey they must have taken, had lost the dignity of things belonging to Amalia. I wanted to try to restore it to them. But the old woman, encouraged by my submissive tones, undid the chain from the door, and stepped into the doorway.

"In any case," she said, "at this hour I'm not going to go back to sleep."

I was afraid that she wanted to come into the house and withdrew quickly toward my mother's apartment.

"I, on the other hand, am going to try to sleep a little," I said.

Signora De Riso darkened and immediately stopped following me. She put the chain back on the door with contempt.

"Amalia, too, always wanted to come to my house and never asked me into hers," she muttered. Then she closed the door in my face.

8.

I sat down on the floor and started with the suitcase. I opened it but found nothing that I could recognize as belonging to my mother. Everything was brand-new: a pair of pink slippers, a robe of ivory satin, two dresses that had never been worn, one of a rusty red too tight for her and too youthful, one quieter, blue, but quite short, five pairs of expensive underpants, a brown leather beauty case full of perfumes, deodorants, creams, makeup, cleansers—she had never used makeup in her life.

I went on to the purse. The first thing I took out was a pair of white lace underpants. I was convinced immediately by the three "V"s clearly visible on the right and from the stylish design that they were the companion of the bra that Amalia was wearing when she drowned. I examined them carefully: they had a little tear on the left side, as if they had been put on even though they were clearly a size too small. I felt my stomach contract and I held my breath. Then I rummaged in the purse again, looking first for the house keys. Naturally I didn't find them. I found instead her reading glasses, nine telephone tokens, and her wallet. In the wallet were two hundred and twenty thousand lire (a sizable amount for her: she lived on the little money that we three sisters sent her every month), the receipt for the electricity bill, her identity card in a plastic case, an old photograph of my sisters and me with our father. The photograph was ruined. Those images of us from so long ago were yellowed, cracked, like the figures of winged demons in certain altarpieces that the faithful have defaced with pointed objects.

I left the photograph on the floor and got up, fighting a growing nausea. I looked through the house for a telephone book and, when I found it, turned quickly to Caserta. I didn't want to telephone him: I wanted the address. When I discovered that there were three densely printed pages of Casertas I realized that I didn't even know what his name was: no one, in the course of my childhood, had ever called him anything but Caserta. So I threw the phone book in a corner and went into the bathroom. I couldn't hold back the retching, and for a few seconds I was afraid that my whole body would be unleashed against me, with a self-destructive fury that as a child I had always feared and, growing up, had tried to control. Then I calmed down. I rinsed out my mouth and washed my face carefully. Seeing it pale and un-made-up in the mirror tilted over the sink I decided to put on makeup.

It was an unusual reaction. I didn't wear makeup often or willingly. I had worn it as a girl but for a long time I hadn't used any: it didn't seem to me that makeup improved me. But just then I seemed to need it. I took the beauty case from my mother's suitcase, went back to the bathroom, opened it, took out a jar of moisturizing cream whose surface bore the timid imprint of Amalia's finger. I erased the trace of hers with my own and used it generously. I rubbed the cream into the skin energetically, smoothing my cheeks. Then, with the powder, I meticulously covered my face.

"You're a ghost," I said to the woman in the mirror. She had the face of a person in her forties, she closed first one eye, then the other, drawing a black pencil over each. She was thin, angular, with prominent cheekbones, the skin miraculously unlined. Her hair was cut very short in order to display as little of its black color as possible, although, to my relief, the black was finally fading to gray and preparing to disappear forever. I put on the mascara.

"I don't look like you," I whispered as I put on some blusher. And in order not to be contradicted, I tried not to look at her. So, in the mirror, I caught sight of the bidet. I turned to see what was missing from that old-fashioned object, with its giant, encrusted taps, and when I realized it I felt like laughing. Caserta had taken even the blood-stained underpants that I had left on the floor.

9.

The coffee was almost ready when I arrived at Uncle Filippo's. With only one arm, he managed mysteriously to do everything. He had an antiquated coffee maker of the type in use before the *moka* espresso maker established itself in every house. It was a metal cylinder with a spout that, disassembled, was divided into four parts: a container for boiling the water, a compartment for the ground coffee, the perforated screw-on top, a pot. When I entered the kitchen, the hot water was already dripping into the pot and an intense smell of coffee was spreading through the apartment.

"How well you look," he said, but I don't think he was alluding to the makeup. He had never seemed to me capable of distinguishing between a made-up woman and one who was not. He meant only that I looked particularly good that morning. In fact, while he was sipping the boiling-hot coffee, he added: "Of the three of you, you look most like Amalia."

I gave a hint of a smile. I didn't want to alarm him by telling him what had happened to me during the night. Nor did I want to start discussing my resemblance to Amalia. It was seven in the morning and I was tired. Half an hour earlier I had cut across the half-deserted Via Foria, the sounds of the city still so faint that it was possible to hear the birds sing. There was a cool breeze, which seemed fresh, and a foggy light wavering between good weather and bad. But on Via Duomo the sounds intensified, along with the voices of women in their houses; the air became grayer and heavier. I had turned up at Uncle Filippo's with a big plastic bag in which I had put the contents of my mother's suitcase and purse, and had surprised him with his trousers unbuttoned and sagging, an undershirt on his bony torso, the stump of his arm bare. He had opened the windows and immediately tidied himself. Then he had begun to press me with offers of nourishment. Did I want fresh bread, did I want milk to dip it in?

I didn't wait to be persuaded and began to nibble this and that. He had been a widower for six years, he lived alone like all old people without children, and didn't sleep much. He was happy to have me there, in spite of the early morning hour, and I was happy myself to be there. I wanted a few moments of peace, the things I had left at his house for the past few days, a change of clothes. I intended to go right away to the Vossi sisters' shop. But Uncle Filippo was eager for company and for talk. He threatened Caserta with horrible deaths. He hoped that he had died a painful death already, during the night. He regretted not having killed him in the past. And then, through a series of connections difficult to disentangle, he began to jump from one family story to another, in a thick dialect. He barely stopped to catch his breath.

After a few attempts I gave up interrupting him. He muttered, he got angry, his eyes became bright with tears, he sniffed. When the monologue turned to Amalia, he went in a few minutes from melancholy praise of his sister to pitiless criticism of the fact that she had abandoned my father. He even forgot to speak of her in the past and began to reproach her as if she were still alive and present or about to emerge from the other room. Amalia, he began to shout, never thinks of the consequences ahead of time: she was always like that, she should have sat down and reflected and waited; instead she woke up one morning and left the house along with you three girls. She shouldn't have done it, according to Uncle Filippo. I soon realized that he wanted to trace back to that separation twenty-three years earlier his sister's decision to drown herself.

Ridiculous. I was annoyed but let him go on, especially since every so often he paused and, changing his hostile tone to one of affection, eagerly took from the cupboard more tins: mint candies, old biscuits, some blackberry jam white with mold but according to him still good.

While I tried to refuse these offerings and then in resignation ate, he started off again, confusing dates and facts. Was it '46 or '47—he tried to remember. Then he changed his mind and concluded: after the war. It was Caserta who, after the war, had realized that my father's talent could be used to improve life a little. Without Caserta, it had to be admitted, in all honesty, my father would have continued to paint, for almost nothing, mountains, moons, palm trees, and camels in the neighborhood shops. Instead, Caserta, who was a crafty fellow, black, black as a Moor but with the eyes of a devil, had begun to do business with the American sailors. Not selling women or other goods but in particular pursuing the sailors who were suffering from homesickness. And instead of showing them photographs of women for sale, he worked on them, urging them to take out of their wallets the photographs of the women they had left at home. Once he had transformed the sailors into abandoned and anxious children, he made a deal on the price and brought the photos to my father, who would make oil portraits from them.

I, too, remembered those images. My father had done them for years, even without Caserta. It seemed that the sailors, with their endless sighs, had nearly worn away the paper images of their women. They were pictures of mamas, of sisters, of fiancées, all blond, all smiling, all photographed with permanents, not a hair out of place, jewels at their necks and ears. They seemed to be dolls. And also, as in the picture of us that Amalia treasured, as in every photograph corroded by absence, the patina of the print was faded and the image often folded at the corners or disfigured by white creases that cut across faces, dresses, necklaces, hairdos. They were faces dying even in the fantasies of those who held on to them with desire and a sense of guilt. My father took them from Caserta's hands and attached them to the easel with a thumbtack. In less than no time, a woman emerged on the canvas who seemed real, a mother-sister-wife who sighed instead of causing sighs. The creases disappeared, the black and white became color, flesh. And the makeup of that aid to memory was applied with a skill sufficient to satisfy men who were lost and unhappy. Caserta came by to pick up the goods, left some money, and went off.

Thus, my uncle recounted, in a short time life changed. Thanks to the women of the American sailors, we ate every day. And he did, too, because he had been unemployed at the time. My mother gave him some money, but with the consent of my father. Or perhaps secretly. Anyway, after years of privation, things were getting better. If Amalia had been more attentive to consequences, if she hadn't gotten mixed up in it, who knows where it would have led. Very far, according to my uncle.

I thought of that money and of my mother as she appeared in the photographs in the family album: eighteen, her stomach already arced by my presence inside her, standing outside on a balcony; part of her Singer could always be seen in the background. She must have stopped pedaling the sewing machine only to be photographed; I was sure that then, after that moment, she had gone back to work, bending over the machine, with no photograph to record her in that misery of common labor, no smile, no sparkling eyes, no hair arranged to make her more beautiful. I think that Uncle Filippo had never thought of the contribution of Amalia's work. I had never thought about it myself. I shook my head, unhappy with myself: I hated talk of the past. For that reason, as long as I lived with Amalia I had seen my father no more than ten times in all, forced to by her. And, since I had been living in Rome, only twice, or three times. He still lived in the house where I was born: two rooms and a kitchen. He spent the whole day sitting there, painting ugly scenes of the bay or crude stormy seas for country fairs. That was how he had always earned his living, getting a little money from middlemen like that Caserta; and I had never liked seeing him chained to the repetition of the same gestures, the same colors, the same shapes, the same odors that I had known since childhood. Above all I couldn't bear him revealing to me his muddle of excuses, as, meanwhile, he piled insults on Amalia, without granting her any virtues.

No, I no longer liked anything about the past. I had made a clean break with all my relatives in order to avoid, at every encounter, hearing them lament in their dialect the evil misfortune of my mother and make vulgar threats toward my father. Only Uncle Filippo remained. I had seen him over the years not by choice but only because he would show up unexpectedly at our house and quarrel with his sister. He did it vehemently, in a loud voice, and then they made up. Amalia was very attached to her only brother, not good for much, the slave since he was a young man of her husband and Caserta. And in some ways she was happy that he continued to see my father and came and told her how he was, what he was doing, what he was working on. I, however—although I felt an ancient sympathy for that depleted body and that boastful, gangsterish aggressiveness, and although, if I had wanted, I could have knocked him to the ground with a fist—would have preferred that he, too, fade away, as so many uncles and great-aunts had. I had trouble accepting that he put my father in the right and her in the wrong. He was her brother, a hundred times he had seen her battered by slaps, punches, kicks; and yet he had never lifted a finger to help her. For forty years he had continued steadfastly to declare solidarity with his brother-in-law. Only in the past few years had I been able to listen to him without getting upset. As a girl I couldn't bear that alliance. After a while I would put my fingers in my ears in order not to hear him. Maybe I couldn't tolerate that the most secret part of myself used that solidarity to give weight to a hypothesis cultivated with equal secrecy: that my mother bore inscribed in her body a natural guilt, independent of her will and of what she really did, and yet readily appearing as needed in every gesture, in every breath. "Is this your shirt?" I asked him, to change the subject, taking from one of the plastic bags the blue shirt I had found in Amalia's house. So I cut him off, and he was for a moment disoriented, eyes wide and lips half-closed. Then, annoyed, he examined the garment at length. But he saw little or nothing without his glasses: he looked at the shirt just to calm himself after his anger, and give an appearance of control.

"No," he said. "Never owned a shirt like that."

I told him I had found it in Amalia's house among the dirty clothes. It was a mistake.

"Whose is it?" he asked, starting to get agitated again, as if I had not been trying to find out the same thing from him. I tried to explain that I didn't know, but it was useless. He gave me back the shirt as if he considered it contagious and began again to criticize his sister remorselessly.

"She was always like that," he said, returning to dialect and growing enraged. "You remember the business of the fruit that came to the house every day? It came out of the blue: she did-n't know how or when. And the book of poetry with the inscription? And the flowers? And the *sfogliatelle* every day at eight o'clock sharp? And the dress, do you remember that? Is it possible you don't remember anything? Who bought her that dress, just her size? She said she didn't know anything about it. But she put it on to go out, secretly, without saying anything to your father. Explain to me why she did that."

I realized that he continued to think that Amalia's behavior was subtly ambiguous, even when my father had grabbed her by the neck and the livid marks of his fingers remained on her skin. She'd say to us, her daughters: "He's like that. He does-n't know what he's doing and I don't know what to tell him." We, on the other hand, thought that our father, because of everything he did to her, should leave the house one morning and be burned to death or crushed or drowned. We thought it and hated her, because she was the linchpin of these thoughts. About this we had no doubts and I had not forgotten it.

I had forgotten nothing but I didn't want to remember. If

necessary, I could have told myself everything, in every detail; but why do it? I told myself only what was useful, according to the situation, deciding from moment to moment on the wave of necessity. Now, for example, I saw the peaches trampled on the floor, the roses slammed ten, twenty times against the kitchen table, the red petals scattering everywhere through the air, the thorny stems still wrapped in silver paper, the pastries dumped out the window, the dress burned on the kitchen stove. I smelled the sickening odor that fabric gives off when one absentmindedly leaves the hot iron on it, and I was afraid.

"No, you don't remember, any of you, you don't know anything," said my uncle, as if I represented, at that moment, my two sisters as well. And he wanted to force me to remember: didn't we know that my father began to beat her only when he wanted to give up Caserta and the portraits for the Americans, and she opposed him? It wasn't something Amalia should have interfered in. But she had the vice of meddling in everything, without thinking. My father had invented a Gypsy woman who danced naked. He had shown her to the head of a network of peddlers who worked the city streets and the countryside selling landscapes and seascapes. The man was called Migliaro, and always brought along his son, who had crooked teeth, and he had judged that it would be successful in doctors' and dentists' offices. He had said that he was willing to give a much higher percentage for those Gypsies than what Caserta was giving him. But Amalia was against it, she didn't want him to leave Caserta, she didn't want him to paint the Gypsies, she didn't even want him to show them to Migliaro.

"You don't remember and you don't know," Uncle Filippo repeated, bitterly, because those times had vanished which had seemed to him good, and they had gone without bearing the promised fruit.

Then I asked him what had happened to Caserta after the break with my father. Many possible furious answers passed through his eyes. Then he decided to abandon the most violent, and asserted proudly that they had given Caserta what he deserved.

"You told your father everything. Your father called me and we went to murder him. If he had tried to react, we really would have killed him."

Everything. Me. I didn't like that suggestion and didn't want to know what "you" he was talking about. I cancelled out every sound that stood in for my name as if it were not possible to allude to me in any way. He looked at me questioningly and, seeing me impassive, shook his head again in disapproval.

"You remember nothing," he repeated, discouraged. And he went on to tell me about Caserta. Afterward, he was frightened and had understood. He had sold a half-failing *bar-pasticceria* that was his father's and left the neighborhood with his wife and son. After a while a rumor had surfaced that he was a receiver of stolen medicines. Then it was said that he had invested the money from that trafficking in a print shop. Strange, because he wasn't a printer. The hypothesis of Uncle Filippo was that he printed covers for pirated records. Anyway, at some point a fire had destroyed the print shop and Caserta had been in the hospital for a while because of burns he had suffered on his legs. From that time on, Filippo didn't know anything about him. Some thought that he had gotten rich thanks to the money from the insurance, and so had gone to live in another city. Others said that after he was burned he had gone from doctor to doctor, and had never been cured: not because of the injury to his legs but because he had a screw loose. He had always been a strange man: it was said that as he grew old he became even stranger. That was it. Uncle Filippo didn't know anything else about Caserta.

I asked him what his name was: I had looked in the phone book but there were too many Casertas.

"Don't you dare look for him," he said, growling again.

"I'm not looking for Caserta," I lied. "I want to see Antonio, his son. We used to play together as children."

"It's not true. You want to see Caserta."

"I'll ask my father," it occurred to me to say.

He looked at me in amazement, as if I were Amalia.

"You do it on purpose," he muttered. And said in a low voice: "Nicola. His name was Nicola. But it's pointless to look in the phone book: Caserta is a nickname. His actual last name I have here in my head but I don't remember it."

He seemed really to concentrate, to please me, but then he gave up, depressed: "Forget it, go back to Rome. If you really intend to see your father, at least don't tell him about this shirt. Even today for a thing like that he would kill your mother."

"He can't do anything to her anymore," I reminded him. But, as if he hadn't heard, he asked:

"Do you want more coffee?"

10.

I gave up on changing my clothes, and stayed in my dusty, wrinkled dark dress. I could barely find the time to change my tampon. Uncle Filippo, with his attentions and his angry outbursts, didn't leave me alone for a minute. When I said that I had to go to the Vossi sisters' shop to buy some underwear, he was bewildered, and remained silent for a few seconds. Then he offered to go with me to the bus.

The day was airless, and getting darker, and the bus turned out to be crowded. Uncle Filippo appraised the crowd and decided to get on, too, to protect me—he said—from purse snatchers and hoodlums. By some lucky circumstance a seat became free: I told him to sit down but he refused vigorously. I sat down myself and an exhausting journey began, through a city without colors, choked by traffic. There was a strong odor of ammonia in the bus, and hanging in the air a fine dust that at some point had come in through the open windows. It tickled your nose. My uncle managed to start an argument first with a man who had not moved aside quickly enough when, to get to the seat that was free, I had asked to get by, and then with a youth who was smoking even though it wasn't allowed. Both treated him with a menacing scorn that took no account of his seventy years or his stump of an arm. I heard him curse and threaten, while he was pushed by the crowd far from me, toward the center of the bus.

I began to sweat. I was squeezed between two old women who stared straight ahead with an unnatural rigidity. One held her purse tight under her arm; the other pressed hers against her stomach, one hand on the clasp, the thumb in a ring attached to the pull of the zipper. The passengers who were standing leaned over us, breathing on us. Women suffocated between male bodies, panting because of that accidental closeness, irritating even if apparently guiltless. In the crush men used the women to play silent games with themselves. One stared ironically at a dark-haired girl to see if she would lower her gaze. One, with his eyes, caught a bit of lace between two buttons of a blouse, or harpooned a strap. Others passed the time looking out the window into cars for a glimpse of an uncovered leg, the play of muscles as a foot pushed brake or clutch, a hand absentmindedly scratching the inside of a thigh. A small thin man, crushed by those behind him, tried to make contact with my knees and nearly breathed in my hair.

I turned toward the nearest window, in search of air. When as a child I had made that same trip, by tram, with my mother, the vehicle climbed the hill with a sort of painful braying sound, like a donkey, among old gray buildings, until a strip of the sea appeared on which I imagined the tram would set sail. The panes of glass vibrated in their wooden frames. The floor also vibrated, sending up through the body a pleasant tremor that I let extend to my teeth, relaxing my jaws just slightly to feel how the top teeth jiggled against the bottom.

It was a journey I liked, going up in the tram, and returning in the funicular: the same slow, unfrenzied mechanisms, and just the two of us, my mother and me. Above, attached to the handrail by leather straps, swung massive handles. If you grabbed onto one, the weight of your body made the writing and colored drawings in the metal block above the handles jump, so that with every jerk the letters and images changed. The handles advertised shoe polish, shoes, various goods of local shops. If the tram wasn't crowded, Amalia left some of her brown paper packages on the seat and held me up so I could play with the handles.

But if the tram was crowded, every pleasure was precluded. Then I was possessed by a mania to protect my mother from any contact with men, as I had seen my father do in the same situation. I placed myself like a shield behind her, crucified myself to her legs, my forehead against her buttocks, arms outstretched, one hand tight on the iron support of the seat on the right, the other on that of the left.

It was wasted effort, Amalia's body couldn't be contained. Her hips spread across the aisle toward the hips of the men on either side of her; her legs, her stomach swelled toward the knee or shoulder of whoever was sitting in front of her. Or maybe it was the opposite. Maybe it was the men who pasted themselves to her, like flies to the sticky yellowish paper that hung in butcher shops or, loaded with dead insects, dangled over the counters of the *salumieri*. It was hard to keep the men away with knees or elbows. They caressed my head lightly and said to my mother: "This pretty little girl's getting crushed." Someone even wanted to pick me up, but I refused. My mother laughed and said: "Come on, come here." I resisted, anxiously. I felt that if I yielded they would take her away and I would be left alone with my angry father.

He protected her from other men violently, but whether it was a violence that would crush only rivals or would be turned against himself, fatally, I never knew. He was an unsatisfied man. Maybe he had not always been but had become so since he had stopped roaming the neighborhood, getting along by decorating shop counters or carts in exchange for food, and had ended up painting, on canvases not yet fixed to frames, landscapes, seascapes, still-lifes, exotic lands, and armies of Gypsies. Who knows what destiny he had imagined for himself; he was furious because life didn't change, because Amalia didn't believe that it would change, because people didn't appreciate him as they should. He repeated constantly, to convince himself and to convince her, that my mother had been very lucky in marrying him. She was so dark you didn't know what blood she came from. He, however, who was fair and blond, felt in his blood something special. Although he stuck unrelentingly to the same colors, the same subjects, the same countryside, and the same sea, he fantasized without restraint about his abilities. We, his daughters, were ashamed of him and believed that he might hurt us as he threatened to do to anyone who touched our mother. When he was on the tram, too, we were afraid. In particular, he kept an eye on short, dark, curly-haired men, with thick lips. He attributed to that anthropological type a desire to steal Amalia's body; but perhaps he thought that it was my mother who was attracted by those square, strong restless bodies. Once he was certain that a man in the crowd had touched her. In front of everyone he slapped her: in front of us. I was painfully astonished. I was sure that he would kill the man, and I didn't understand why, instead, he hit her. Even now I didn't know why he had done it. Maybe to punish her for having felt in the fabric of her dress, on her skin, the warmth of that other body.

11.

With the bus unmoving in the chaos of Via Salvator Rosa, I discovered that I no longer felt any sympathy for the city of Amalia, for the language in which she spoke to me, for the streets that I had walked as a girl, for the people. When at a certain point there appeared a glimpse of the sea (the same that had excited me as a child), it seemed to me purple parchment pasted over a crack in a wall. I knew that I was losing my mother definitively and that it was exactly what I wanted.

The Vossi sisters' shop was in Piazza Vanvitelli. As a girl I had often stopped in front of the sober windows, their thick panes of glass enclosed in mahogany frames. The entrance had an old door whose upper part was glass, and at the top were incised the three "V"s and the date of the shop's founding, 1948. I didn't know what was beyond the glass, which was opaque: I had never had either the need to go and see or the money to do so. I had often stopped outside because I especially liked the corner window, where women's garments were carelessly placed beneath a painting that I wasn't able to date, but that was certainly by a skilled artist. Two women, so close and so identical in movement that their profiles were almost superimposed, were running openmouthed, from the right side of the canvas to the left. You couldn't tell if they were following or being followed. The image seemed to have been cut away from a much larger scene, and so only the left legs of the women were visible and their extended arms were severed at the wrists. Even my father, who had some objection or other to every painting that had been made in the course of the centuries, liked it. He invented stupid attributions, pretending to be an expert, as if we all didn't know that he hadn't been to any kind of school, that of art he knew little or nothing, that all he could paint, night and day, was his Gypsies. When he was in the mood and disposed to boast more than usual with us, his daughters, he even attributed it to himself.

It was at least twenty years since I had had occasion to go up the hill, to this place near the castle of San Martino that I recalled as cool and clean, different from the rest of the city. I was immediately vexed. The piazza seemed to me changed, with its few spindly plane trees, encroached on by the steel bodies of cars, and overhung by a scaffolding of yellow-painted iron beams. I recalled that at the center of the piazza of long ago were palm trees that had seemed to me very tall. There was one, a sickly dwarf, besieged by the gray barriers of the construction. Furthermore, I couldn't at first glance find the shop. Tailed by my uncle, who was continuing with himself the argument he had been having with the people on the bus, even though it had occurred an hour earlier, I circled the space: dust-filled, noisy, bombarded by horns and pneumatic drills, beneath a cloudy sky that seemed to want to rain and couldn't. Finally I stopped in front of some wigless female mannequins in underpants and bras, carefully positioned in bold, even vulgar, attitudes. Among mirrors, gilded bits of metal, and fabrics in electric colors, I had difficulty recognizing the three "V"s in the arch of the door, the only thing that remained the same. Even the painting I liked was no longer there.

I looked at my watch: it was ten-fifteen. The activity was such that the whole piazza—buildings, gray-violet colonnades, clouds of sounds and dust—seemed a merry-go-round. Uncle Filippo glanced at the display windows and immediately turned away in embarrassment: too many spread legs, too many provocative breasts, he'd have ugly thoughts. He said that he would wait for me on the corner: that I should be quick. I said to myself that I hadn't asked him to come with me, and I went in.

I had always imagined that, inside, the Vossi sisters' shop was dim, and inhabited by three genteel old ladies, wearing long dresses and thick strands of pearls, their hair gathered in chignons held by old-fashioned hairpins. Instead I found bright lights, loud customers, mannequins in satin nightgowns, camisoles in many colors, silk underpants, counters and tables that overloaded the place with merchandise, heavily made-up young salesgirls, all wearing tight pistachio-colored uniforms with the three "V"s embroidered on the chest.

"Is this the Vossi sisters' shop?" I asked one of them, the one who looked the nicest, perhaps uneasy in her uniform.

"Yes. May I help you?"

"Could I speak with one of the Miss Vossis?"

The girl looked at me, bewildered.

"They're not here anymore," she said.

"Are they dead?"

"No, I don't think so. They've retired."

"Did they give up the shop?"

"They were getting on, they sold everything. There's new management now, but the label is the same. Are you an old customer?"

"My mother was," I said. And I slowly began to take from the plastic bag that I had brought with me the nightgown, the two dresses, the five pairs of underpants found in Amalia's suitcase, spreading out everything on the counter. "I think she bought them all here."

The girl looked with expert eyes.

"The things, yes, they're ours," she said with a questioning air. I saw that she was trying to guess my mother's age based on how old I seemed to be.

"She'll be sixty-three in July," I said. Then it occurred to me to lie: "They weren't for her. They were gifts for me, for my birthday. I was forty-five on May 23rd."

"You look at least fifteen years younger," the girl said, trying to do her job.

In an engaging tone, I explained:

"The things are beautiful, and I like them. Only, this dress binds a little and the panties are tight."

"Do you want to exchange them? I'd need the receipt."

"I don't have the receipt. But they were bought here. Don't you remember my mother?"

"I don't know. So many people come here."

I glanced at the people the salesgirl had alluded to: women who talked loudly in a dialect marked by a forced cheer, who laughed noisily, flaunted expensive jewelry, came out of the fitting rooms in bra and underpants or in tiny gold, silver, or leopard-print bathing suits, displayed abundant flesh striped by stretch marks and dented by cellulite, gazed at pubis and buttocks, pushed their breasts up with cupped hands, ignored the saleswomen, and, in those poses, turned to a man who was a kind of floorwalker, well dressed and already tanned, installed there purposely to channel the flow of money and cast threatening glances at the ineffectual salesgirls.

It wasn't the clientele I had imagined. They seemed women whose men had got rich suddenly and easily, hurling them into a provisional luxury that they were compelled to enjoy, and whose subculture was like a damp crowded basement, with semi-porn comic strips, with obscenities used as refrains. They were women forced into a city-prison, corrupted first by poverty and now by money, with no interruption. Seeing them and hearing them, I realized that I was getting nervous. They behaved with that man the way my father imagined women behaved, the way he imagined his wife behaved as soon as he turned his back, the way Amalia, too, perhaps, had for her whole life dreamed of behaving: a woman of the world who bends over without having to place two fingers at the center of her neckline, crosses her legs without worrying about her skirt, laughs coarsely, covers herself with costly objects, her whole body brimming with indiscriminate sexual offerings, ready to joust face to face with men in the arena of the obscene.

I made an uncontrollable grimace of annoyance. I said:

"She's the same height as I am, with only a little white in her hair. But she wears it in an old-fashioned style, no one does it like that anymore. She came with a man of about seventy, but pleasant, slender, with thick white hair. A handsome couple, to look at. You ought to remember them, they bought all these things."

The salesgirl shook her head, she didn't remember.

"So many people come here," she said. Then she glanced at the floorwalker, worried about the time she was wasting, and suggested to me: "Try them on. They look just your size. If the dress is tight . . . "

"I'd like to speak to that man . . . " I ventured.

The salesgirl pushed me toward a fitting room, anxious about that barely articulated request.

"If the underpants don't fit, take another pair . . . we'll give you a discount," she offered. And I found myself in a tiny room that was all rectangular mirrors.

I sighed, and wearily took off the funeral dress. I had less and less tolerance for the frenetic chatter of the customers, which in there seemed not muffled but, rather, amplified. After a moment of hesitation I also took off the underpants of my mother's that I had put on the night before and changed into the lace ones that I had found in her bag. They were exactly my size. Puzzled, I ran a finger along the rip in the side that Amalia had probably made putting them on and then pulled over my head the rust-colored dress. It came to about two inches above my knees and the neckline was too low. But it wasn't at all too tight; rather, it slid over my tense and muscular thinness and softened it. I came out of the fitting room tugging the dress on one side, staring at one calf and saying aloud:

"Look, you can see, the dress is tight here on the side . . . and anyway it's too short."

But beside the young salesgirl now was the man, who appeared to be in his forties, with a black mustache, at least eight inches taller than me, broad in the shoulders and chest.

Both his features and his body were inflated, threatening; only his gaze was not unpleasant but lively, familiar. He said, in a TV Italian, but without kindness, without even a hint of the willing compliance that he showed with the other customers, in fact visibly striving to be formal with me:

"It looks very good on you, it's not at all too tight. That's the style."

"It's precisely the style that I'm not sure about. My mother chose it without me . . . "

"She made a good choice. Keep your dress and enjoy it."

I stared at him for a second, in silence. I felt that I wanted to do something either to him or to myself. I glanced at the other customers. I pulled the dress up over my hips and turned toward one of the mirrors.

"Look at the panties," I pointed to the mirror, "they're tight on me."

The man changed neither his expression nor his tone.

"Madam, I don't know what to tell you, you don't even have the receipt," he said.

I saw myself in the mirror, my legs thin and bare: I pulled down the dress, uneasy. I picked up the old dress and the underpants, put everything in the bag and searched at the bottom for the plastic case with Amalia's identification card.

"You ought to remember my mother," I tried again, pulling out the document and opening it right in front of him.

The man gave a quick look and seemed to lose patience. He switched to dialect.

"My dear lady, we can't waste time here," he said, and gave back the document.

"I'm only asking you . . . "

"Merchandise that's been sold can't be exchanged."

"I'm only asking you . . . "

He advanced to a light touch on the shoulder.

"Are you playing games? Did you come to play games?"

"Don't you dare touch me . . . "

"No, you really are joking . . . go on, take your things and your document. Who sent you? What do you want? Tell whoever sent you to come and get the cash personally. Then we'll see! In fact, here's my card: Antonio Polledro, name, address, and telephone number. You'll find me here or at home. All right?"

It was a tone that I knew very well. Immediately afterward he would begin to push me harder and then to strike me, without regard to whether I was a man or a woman. I tore the document from his hand with calculated disdain, and to discover what had so unnerved him I looked at the photograph of my mother. The long, baroquely sculpted hair on her forehead and around her face had been carefully scraped away. The white that emerged around her head had been changed with a pencil to a nebulous gray. With the same pencil someone had slightly hardened the features of her face. The woman in the photograph wasn't Amalia: it was me.

12.

I went out into the street carrying my things. I realized that I still had the identity card in my hand, and I put it back in the plastic case, automatically sticking Polledro's card in with it. I slipped everything into my purse and looked around in a daze, glad that Uncle Filippo really had waited for me at the corner.

I immediately regretted it. His eyes widened and his mouth gaped, revealing his few long, nicotine-stained teeth. He was astonished, but astonishment was quickly turning into antagonism. I couldn't immediately understand why. Then I realized that it was the dress I was wearing. I made an effort to smile at him, certainly to calm him down but also to get rid of the impression that I had lost control of my face, that I had a face that had been adapted from Amalia's.

"Does it look bad?" I asked.

"No," he said sulkily, clearly lying.

"Then what?"

"We buried your mother yesterday," he complained in a voice that was too loud.

I thought of revealing, just to annoy him, that the dress was actually Amalia's but foresaw in time that it was I who would be annoyed: he would surely start railing against his sister again.

"I was depressed and I wanted to give myself a present."

"You women get depressed too easily," he burst out, suddenly forgetting, with that "too easily," what he had just reminded me of: that we had a short time ago buried my mother and I had good reason to be depressed.

On the other hand I wasn't really depressed. I felt, rather, as if I had left myself somewhere and was no longer able to find myself: I was worn out, that is, by movements that were too quick and barely coordinated, by the urgency of one who is searching everywhere and has no time to waste. I thought that a cup of chamomile would do me good and I pushed Uncle Filippo into the first bar we came to in Via Scarlatti, while he began to talk about his wife, who was always sad: stern, hard-working, careful, methodical, but sad. But the close space of the bar had the effect of a cotton ball in my mouth. The intense smell of coffee and the loud voices of the customers and barmen drove me back toward the door, while my uncle was already shouting, with his hand in the inside pocket of his jacket, "I'll pay!" I sat down at a table on the sidewalk, amid the squeal of brakes, an odor of imminent rain and of gas, overcrowded buses moving at a walk, people hurrying by and bumping against the table. "I'll pay," Uncle Filippo repeated in a lower voice, even though we hadn't ordered and I doubted that a waiter would ever appear. Then he settled onto the chair and began to praise himself. "I have always been the energetic type. No money? No money. No arm? No arm. No women? No women. What's essential is the mouth and the legs: to speak when you want and to go where you want. Am I right or not?"

"Yes."

"Your mother is like that, too. We are a family that doesn't get discouraged. When she was little, she was constantly bruising herself but she never cried: our mother had taught us to blow on the hurt and say: it will pass. Even when she was working and pricked herself with a needle, she kept this habit of saying: it will pass. Once, the sewing-machine needle pierced the nail of her index finger, came out the other side, went up and in again, three or four times. Well, she stopped the pedal, then started it up, but just enough so she could get the needle out, bandaged the finger, and went back to work. I never saw her sad."

That was all I heard. It seemed to me that I was sinking up to my neck into the window behind me. Even the red wall of the UPIM store across the street seemed freshly coated, the paint still wet. I let the sounds of Via Scarlatti get louder, until they covered his voice. I saw his lips moving, in profile, soundless; they seemed made of rubber, manipulated by two fingers inside. He was seventy and had no reason to be satisfied with himself, but he tried to be, and perhaps he really was when he started off on that ceaseless chatter which was rapidly produced by the almost imperceptible movements of his lips. For a moment I thought with horror of males and females as living organisms, and I imagined the work of a burin polishing us like ivory, reducing us until we were without holes and without excrescences, all identical and without identity, with no play of somatic features, no weighting of small differences.

My mother's wounded finger, pierced by the needle before she was ten, was more familiar to me than my own fingers precisely because of that detail. It was purple, and the nail appeared to sink into the crescent. For a long time I'd wanted to lick it and suck it, more than her nipples. Maybe she had even let me when I was still very small. On the pad of the finger there was a white scar: the wound had become infected, it had had to be lanced. Around it I could smell the odor of her old Singer, which had the shape of an elegant animal, half dog half cat, and the odor of the cracked leather cord that transmitted the action of the pedal from the big wheel to the small one, the needle that went up and down from the animal's muzzle, the thread that ran through its nostrils and ears, the spool that rotated on the pivot fixed to its back. I could smell the oil that was used to grease it, the black paste of oil mixed with dust that I scratched away with a nail and secretly ate. I intended to make a hole in my finger, too, to make her see that it was risky to deny me what I didn't have.

There were too many stories of the infinite, minuscule differences that made her unreachable, and all together turned her into a being desired in the external world at least as much as I desired her. There had been a time when I imagined biting off that distinctive finger, because I couldn't find the courage to offer mine to the mouth of the Singer. Anything in her that had not been conceded to me I wanted to eliminate from her body. Thus nothing more would be lost or dispersed far from me, because finally everything had been lost already.

Now that she was dead, someone had scraped away her hair and had disfigured her face to fit my body. It had happened after years in which, out of hatred, out of fear, I had wanted to eliminate every root I had in her, even the deepest: her gestures, the inflections of her voice, her way of taking a glass or drinking from a cup, her method of putting on a skirt, as if it were a dress, the arrangement of the objects in her kitchen, in her drawers, how she did her most intimate washing, her taste in food, her dislikes, her enthusiasms, and the language, the city, the rhythms of her breath. All of it remade, so that I could become me and detach myself from her.

On the other hand I hadn't wanted or been able to root anyone in me. Soon I would lose even the possibility of having children. No human being would ever detach itself from me with the anguish with which I had detached myself from her, only because I had never been able to attach myself to her definitively. There would not be anyone more or less between me and another aspect of myself. I would remain me until the end, unhappy, discontent with what I had furtively taken from the body of Amalia. Little, too little, the booty I had managed to seize, tearing it from her blood, her belly, and the measure of her breath, to hide in my body, in the capricious matter of the brain. Insufficient. What an ingenuous and careless sort of makeup, to try to call "I" this forced flight from a woman's body, although I had carried away from it less than nothing! I was no I. And I was confused: I didn't know if what I had been discovering and telling myself, ever since she ceased to exist and couldn't refute it, horrified me or gave me pleasure.

13.

Maybe I came to because of the rain on my face. Or because Uncle Filippo, standing beside me, shook me by the arm with the only hand he had. The fact is that I felt a kind of electric shock and realized that I had fallen asleep.

"It's raining," I mumbled while my uncle continued to tug at me furiously. He was shrieking as if beside himself, but I couldn't understand what he was saying. I felt weak and frightened, I couldn't get up. People were rushing around, looking for shelter. Men shouted or laughed loudly and, running, bumped dangerously into the little table. I was afraid that they would knock me over. One sent the chair that had just been occupied by Uncle Filippo flying. "Nice weather," he said, and went into the bar.

I tried to stand, thinking that my uncle wanted to pull me up. Instead he let go of my arm, stumbled through the crowd, and started yelling astonishing insults from the edge of the sidewalk, pointing with his outstretched arm to the other side of the street, beyond the cars and the packed buses with the rain drumming on their roofs.

I got up, carrying the bag and the purse. I wanted to see whom he was getting mad at, but the traffic created a compact wall of steel plates, and the rain was coming down harder and harder. So I crept along the wall of the building to avoid getting soaked and meanwhile found a gap between the stopped cars and buses. Through it I saw Caserta against the red patch of the UPIM. He was bent almost double, but walking quickly, and looking back continuously as if afraid of being followed. He bumped into passersby but did not seem to realize it, nor did he slow down: leaning forward, his arms swinging, at every collision he pirouetted on himself without stopping, as if he were a silhouette attached to a fulcrum that, by means of a secret mechanism, was rolling rapidly along the pavement. From a distance it seemed that he was singing and dancing but perhaps he was only cursing, gesticulating.

I began to hurry, in order not to lose sight of him, but to do so I was soon forced to abandon any attempt at shelter and move into the open, into the rain, since all the passersby had crowded into doorways, into the fronts of shops, or under cornices and balconies. I saw Caserta hop to avoid plants and vases of flowers displayed on the sidewalk by a florist. He didn't make it, stumbled, ended up against the trunk of a tree. He stopped for a second as if he were pasted to the bark, then tore himself off and began running again. I don't know what he was afraid of. I imagined that he had seen my uncle and had taken off. Maybe the two old men were reproducing as if in a game a scene already played when they were young: one pursued, the other fled. I imagined them coming to blows on the wet pavement, tumbling in one direction, then the other. I didn't know how I would react, what I would do.

At the intersection of Via Scarlatti and Via Luca Giordano I realized that I had lost him. I looked around for Uncle Filippo but didn't see him, either. So I crossed Via Scarlatti, which had become a long question mark of stopped vehicles, to Piazza Vanvitelli, and began to hurry back along the opposite sidewalk to the first cross street. There was thunder but no visible lightning, and the thunderclaps were like dry rips in a piece of fabric. I saw Caserta at the end of Via Merliani, whipped by the rain under the metallic blue and red of a big sign, against the white wall of the Villa Floridiana park. I ran after him but a young man came suddenly out from the shelter of a doorway, grabbed me by one arm, laughing, and said to me in dialect, "What's the rush? Let me dry you off!" The tug was so strong that I felt the pain in my collarbone and slipped on my left leg. I didn't fall, only because I hit a garbage can. I regained my balance and pulled myself free, shouting, to my own amazement, insults in dialect. By the time I, too, had reached the boundary wall of the park, Caserta was almost at the top of the street, a few meters from the funicular station that was being renovated.

I stopped with my heart in my throat. He now advanced, without running, along the row of plane trees, between the cars parked on the right. Still bent double, he was struggling, with an endurance in his legs one would not have suspected in a man of that age. When it seemed that he couldn't take another step, he leaned panting against the barrier surrounding a construction site. I saw his body contort, ending up in a position in which a bar of the scaffolding appeared to be emerging from his white hair. On it hung a sign: "Demolition and reconstruction of the Piazza Vanvitelli station—Funicular of Chiaia." I was certain that he wouldn't have the strength to move, when again something alarmed him. With his shoulder he struck the wall of the enclosure as if he wanted to break it and escape through the breach. I looked to the left, to see who was frightening him: I hoped it was my uncle. It wasn't. Coming from Via Bernini, in the rain, was Polledro, the man from the Vossi shop. He was shouting at him and now he gestured at him to stop, now pointed threateningly with his palm outspread.

Caserta hopped from one foot to the other, looking around for a way out. He seemed to have decided to go back down along Via Cimarosa, but he saw me. Then he stood still, smoothed his hair, and seemed suddenly ready to confront both Polledro and me. He walked with his back to the enclosure of the construction site, then against a parked car. I, too, began to run, just in time to see Polledro move, as if he were skating on the metallic gray of the pavement, a massive yet agile figure against the scaffold of yellow-painted iron bars placed at the entrance of Piazza Vanvitelli. But it was at that point that my uncle reappeared. He emerged from a pizzeria where he had taken shelter. He had seen me arrive and now was running after me stiffly, with quick little steps in the rain. The man from the Vossi sisters' appeared in front of him, and they ended up, inevitably, colliding. After the collision they held each other by the arms, each trying to help the other stay on his feet, and in that way rotated, seeking a point of balance. Caserta took advantage of this to dive into the white light of Via Sanfelice, in the sparkling rain, amid the crowd seeking shelter in the entrance to the funicular.

I gathered what energy I had left and ran after him, into a place thick with people's breath, muddied by the rain, grimy with plaster dust. The funicular was about to depart and the passengers pushed and shoved one another toward the ticket-taking machines. Caserta was already beyond them and was going down the steps, stopping frequently, craning his neck to look behind him, and then suddenly bringing his flushed face to whoever happened to be walking next to him to whisper something. Or maybe he was talking to himself but in a voice that he tried to keep low, waving his right hand up and down with three fingers extended and thumb and index finger joined. He waited for a few seconds, in vain, for an answer. Finally he started down again.

I got a ticket and rushed toward the two luminous yellow cars. I couldn't see which one he had gone into. I went halfway along the second car without finding him, and decided to get on, making my way through the crowd of passengers. The air was heavy and smelled of sweat and wet clothes. I tried to find Caserta. Instead I saw Polledro, who was taking the steps two at a time, followed by my uncle, who was shouting at him. They had just time to get on the first car before the doors closed. After a few seconds they appeared against the rectangle of glass that faced my car: the man from the Vossi shop was looking around in a fury and my uncle was pulling him by one arm. The funicular started off.

14.

The cars were new, very different from those of my childhood. These preserved only the shape, a parallelogram whose entire structure seemed to have been thrust backward by a violent shove from the front. But when the funicular began to descend into the oblique well before it, the squeaks, the vibrations, the jerks returned. Yet the cars on their steel cables slid down the cliff with a velocity that had little to do with the slow, restful pace, punctuated by jolts and thuds, at which they used to run. The vehicle, which had been a circumspect probe under the skin of the hill, seemed to have become a brutal injection into a vein. And with annoyance I felt that it dimmed the memory of those pleasant trips with Amalia, after she had stopped making gloves, and took me along when she delivered to the wealthy clients of the Vomero the garments she had sewed for them. She had dressed and done her hair with care, in order to seem no less a lady than those she worked for. I, on the other hand, was thin and dirty, or at least felt that way. I sat beside her on the wooden seat and held on my knees, carefully arranged so that it wouldn't get creased, the garment she was working on or had just finished, wrapped in packing paper that was fastened at the ends with pins. The package rested on my legs and stomach like a case that contained the smell and warmth of my mother. I felt it in every inch of skin touched by the paper. And that contact produced in me a melancholy languor marked by the jerks of the car.

Now instead I had only an impression of losing altitude, like an aged Alice in pursuit of the White Rabbit. I reacted by detaching myself from the door and making an effort to get to the center of the car. I was in the highest part, in the second compartment. I tried to advance, but the passengers stared at me in irritation, as if there were something ugly in my aspect, and repulsed me antagonistically. I struggled to move, then gave up and looked for Caserta. I could make him out at the end, in the last section, which consisted of a broad platform. He was standing behind a shabby-looking girl of around twenty. I saw him in profile, as I saw the girl. He seemed a peaceful old man in dignified old age, intent on reading a newspaper gray from the rain. He held it in his left hand, folded in fourths, and with his right he held onto the polished metal grip. But I soon realized that, swaying with the movement of the car, he was getting ever closer to the girl's body. Now his back was arched, his legs were slightly spread, his stomach leaned against her buttocks. There was nothing that justified that contact. In spite of the crowding, he had enough space behind him to position himself at a proper distance. But, even when the girl turned with barely concealed rage and then pushed her way forward to escape him, the old man didn't desist. He waited a few seconds before regaining the few inches he had lost, then again joined the blue material of his trousers to her jeans. He received a timid elbow in the ribs but continued impassively to pretend to read, and in fact pressed his stomach against her with greater determination.

I turned to look for my uncle. I saw him in the other car, intent, openmouthed. Polledro, next to him in the crowd, was beating on the glass. Maybe he was trying to attract Caserta's attention. Or mine. He no longer had the irritating air that I had seen in the shop. He seemed a humiliated and anxious boy, forced to be present behind a window at a spectacle that made him suffer. My gaze went from him to Caserta: I was disoriented. It seemed to me that they had the same red plastic mouth, stiff with tension. But I couldn't stabilize that impression. The funicular stopped, with a rocking motion, and I saw that the girl moved in a hurry toward the exit. Caserta, as if stuck to her, followed with back arched and legs spread, to the astonishment and nervous laughs of his traveling companions. The young woman jumped out of the car. The old man hesitated a moment, stopped, and looked up. I thought that he was recalled by Polledro's now frantic pounding. Instead, as if he had always known exactly where I was, he picked me out in the crowd, which was now pointing to him with murmurs of disapproval, and, turning to me with a slightly suggestive look, let me understand that the pantomime he had been enacting had to do with me. Then abruptly he slipped out of the car, like a rebel actor who has decided to stop following the script.

I realized that Polledro, too, was trying to get out. I, in turn, tried to reach the door, but I was too far away and was pushed back by the current of people getting on. The funicular started off again. I looked up and realized that the man from the Vossi sisters' shop hadn't made it, either. But Uncle Filippo had.

15.

In the faces of the old it's difficult to trace the lineaments of their youth. At times we can't even imagine that they had a youth. I realized, as the funicular continued its descent, that a little earlier, with the movement of my gaze from Polledro to Caserta and vice versa, I had composed a third man, who was not Caserta or Polledro. He was a young man, olive-skinned, with black hair and a camel overcoat. That ectoplasm, which immediately dissolved, was the result of a shift of somatic features, as if my gaze had caused an accidental confusion between the cheekbones of Caserta and those of the floor-walker from the Vossi shop, between the mouth of one and that of the other. I reproached myself. I had done too many things that I shouldn't have: I had started running, I had given into anxiety, my frenzy had been excessive. I tried to calm myself.

A few minutes later the station of Chiaia appeared, a dimly lighted concrete bunker. I prepared to get out but I still felt unsettled. Now, in my head, Amalia was, in her turn, staring at that fanciful somatic composition I had made. I resigned myself. She stood there, demanding, in a corner of the old station of forty years earlier. I arranged her better in the background, as if I were working on a puzzle that was not yet identifiable from its details: only her loosened hair, a dark profile in front of three painted wooden figures that perhaps had been there a little less than half a century earlier, advertising clothes. Meanwhile I exited from the car, practically pushed down the steps by impatient passengers. I felt cold in spite of the warm damp air, like that of a greenhouse or a catacomb.

Now Amalia had definitely appeared in full, young and lithe, in a station that, like her, was no longer there. I stopped to give her time to stand and stare, spellbound, at the figures: perhaps a sophisticated couple with a German shepherd on a leash. Yes. They were of cardboard and wood, six feet tall, less than half an inch thick, with supports behind their backs. I chose details at random to color and clothe them. The man, it seemed to me, wore a jacket and checked pants, a camelhair overcoat, a perfectly fitting felt hat; one gloved hand held the other glove. The woman wore perhaps a dark suit with a long scarf of a blue material with a delicately colored pattern: on her head she wore a hat with feathers, and her eyes were deep-set behind the veil. The dog was sitting on his hind feet, ears pricked, close to his master's legs. The three of them, looking healthy and content, stood there in the station, which at that time was gray and dusty, and partitioned by a black grating. A few steps away broad shafts of light fell from between the stairs above, making the green (or red?) of the funicular gleam when it slid slowly out of the tunnel in the hill.

I began to descend the stairway toward the bars of the turn-stile. The rest happened in a very brief but extraordinarily dilated lapse of time. Polledro took me by one hand, awkwardly, just under the wrist. I was certain that it was he even before I turned. I heard him asking me to stop. I didn't. He told me that we knew each other well, that he was the son of Nicola Polledro. Then, in case that information wasn't enough, he added: "The son of Caserta."

I stopped. I even left Amalia standing in front of those figures, her mouth half-open, white teeth lightly veined by lipstick, hesitating between an ironic comment and an expression of wonder. The wood-and-cardboard couple let themselves be admired with detachment, on the left at the foot of the steps. I, who felt that I was present at her side even though I couldn't see myself, thought that the couple were images of the owners of the funicular. People who came from far away: they were so anomalous, so out of place, so different in their magical absorption that they seemed from another country. Forty years earlier, I must have considered them a possibility of flight, the proof that other places existed where we could go, Amalia and I, whenever we wanted. I thought certainly that my mother, too, so intent, was studying how to run away with me. But then the suspicion dawned that she was standing there for other reasons: perhaps only to study the woman's clothes and the way she carried herself. Probably she wanted to re-create them in the clothes she sewed. Or learn to dress that way herself, and stand that way, casually, waiting for the funicular. Now, after many decades, I felt, grieving, that there, in that corner of that station, I had not in any way managed to think her thoughts from within her, from within her breath. Already at that point her voice could say to me only: do this, do that. But I could no longer be part of the cavity that conceived those sounds and decided which ones should sound in the external world and which should remain sounds without sound. This pained me.

Polledro's voice arrived like a jolt against that grief. The station of forty years earlier gave a shudder. The figures turned out to be of colored dust and dissolved. After many years, clothing and poses of that sort had disappeared from the world. The couple had been removed, along with their dog, as if, after waiting in vain, they had grown annoyed and had decided to return to their castle of somewhere or other. I had trouble keeping Amalia standing in front of that void. Furthermore, a moment before Polledro stopped speaking, I had realized that I was confused, that the dark suit of the cardboard woman and her scarf had been not hers but my mother's. It was Amalia who dressed in that elegant fashion, so long ago. As if for an appointment that was important to her. Now with her mouth half-open, teeth lightly veined by the lipstick, she was staring not at the figures but at him, the man in the camelhair coat. And the man spoke to her, and she answered, and he spoke to her again, but I didn't understand what they were saying.

Polledro spoke to me ingratiatingly to force me to listen to him. I looked at him, mesmerized, but I couldn't manage to pay attention. Under the well-fed features he had the face of his father as a young man, and he was helping me, without wanting to, tell myself about Caserta, who was meeting my mother in the damaged station of Chiaia. I shook my head and Polledro must have thought that I didn't believe him. In fact it was in myself that I had no faith. He repeated: "It's me, Antonio, the son of Caserta." I was realizing that all I really preserved of those figures of wood and cardboard was an impression of foreign lands and unkept promises. They gleamed like newly polished shoes, but without details. They could just as easily have been advertising figures of two men, or two women; there might have been no dog; they could have had a lawn under their feet or a sidewalk; and I couldn't even remember what they were advertising. I no longer knew. The details that I had unburied—now I was sure of it—did not belong to them: they were merely the result of a chaotic assemblage of clothing and gestures. The only clear thing now was that handsome young face, olive-skinned, with black hair, the features of Polledro the son superimposed on a shadow that had been Polledro the father. Caserta spoke gently to Amalia, holding his son Antonio by the hand, who was just my age; and my mother held me, certainly without being aware of my hand in hers. I recognized Caserta's mouth, moving quickly, and I saw his red tongue: the frenulum that anchored it kept it from darting toward Amalia more than it already was. I realized that, in my head, the cardboard man of the funicular had worn Caserta's clothes and that his companion had worn my mother's. The hat with feathers and veil had traveled far, from some wedding celebration or other, before coming to rest there. I didn't know the fate of the scarf except that it had remained for years around the neck and shoulders of my mother. As for the suit, it—sewed, taken apart, turned—was the same one that Amalia had worn when she took the train to Rome to celebrate my birthday. How many things pass through time randomly detached from the bodies and voices of persons. My mother knew the art of making clothes last forever.

Finally I said to Polledro, surprising him by the sociable tone that he didn't expect, after so much silent resistance:

"I remember very well. You're Antonio. How in the world did I not recognize you right away? You have the same eyes as before."

I smiled to show that I wasn't hostile but also to find out if he felt hostile toward me. He stared at me in bewilderment. I saw him ready to lean over and kiss me on the cheeks but then he decided not to, as if something about me repelled him.

"What's the matter?" I asked the man from the Vossi sisters', who, now that the tension of approaching me had vanished, looked at me with a kind of irony. "Don't you like my dress anymore?"

After a moment of uncertainty Polledro decided. He smiled and said to me:

"You're a bit of a mess. Have you seen yourself? Come, you can't go around like that."

16.

He pushed me toward the exit and then, quickly, toward the taxi stand. People who had been surprised by the rain were crowding under the roof of the subway entrance. The sky was black and the wind was blowing hard, driving on a diagonal a curtain of fine dense drops. Polledro got me into a taxi reeking of smoke. He spoke with speed and assurance, without leaving me space, as if he were convinced that I must feel great interest in what he was saying. But I was hardly listening; I couldn't concentrate. I had the impression that he lacked a precise plan, that he was talking with a frantic display of self-possession that served only to contain his anxiety. I didn't want it to infect me.

With a certain solemnity he begged my pardon in the name of his father. He said he didn't know what to do: old age had utterly ruined his brain. But he assured me immediately that the old man wasn't dangerous, and that he wasn't bad. He was uncontrollable, yes: he had a strong, healthy body, he was always out and about, it was impossible to restrain him. When he managed to steal enough money from him, he disappeared for months. Abruptly he began to list for me the cashiers he had had to let go because they had been corrupted or taken in by his father.

While Polledro spoke, I noticed his smell: not his true smell, which was overpowered by the stench of sweat and tobacco that pervaded the taxi, but an odor invented by starting from that of the shop selling sweets and spices where we had often played together. The shop belonged to his grandfather and was a few blocks from where my parents lived. The sign was of wood, painted blue, and next to the legend "Coloniali" there was a palm tree and a black woman with very red lips. That sign my father had painted at the age of twenty. He had also painted the counter in the shop. He had used a color called burnt sienna to make a desert, and in the desert he had put a lot of palm trees, two camels, a man in a bush jacket and boots, cascades of coffee, African dancers, an ultramarine-blue sky, and a quarter moon. It was easy to reach that landscape. Children lived out on the street, without supervision: I would leave the courtyard of our building, turn the corner, and push open the wooden door, which had a window in the upper half and a diagonal metal bar across it. Immediately a bell rang. Then I went in and the door closed behind me. The edge was padded with fabric, or perhaps covered with rubber, to keep it from slamming. The air smelled of cinnamon and cream. On the threshold were two sacks with rolled-down edges, full of coffee beans. Above, on the marble counter, containers of cut glass, with designs in relief, displayed white, blue, and red sugared almonds, caramels, multicolored candies that melted in your mouth, releasing onto your tongue a sweet liquid, black licorice in sticks, in coiled or loose laces, in the shape of fish or boats. While the taxi battled the wind, the rain, the flooded streets, the traffic, I couldn't reconcile disgust for Caserta's red tongue, for the scary games played with the child Antonio, for the violence and blood that derived from them, with the faint odor that Polledro preserved in his breath.

Now he was trying to excuse his father. Sometimes—he was saying to me—he bothered people a little, but you just had to have patience; without patience, living in that city was difficult. Especially since the old man didn't do any great harm. The greater harm was not what he did to his neighbor; it was the damage he did at the shop when he bothered the clients. Then it made him see red, and if the old man had fallen into his hands it would have been easy to forget that he was his father. He asked if he had bothered me. Was it possible that he himself hadn't realized I was Amalia's daughter? It had taken him a few moments, the time to collect his thoughts: I couldn't know what a pleasure it was to see me again. He had run after me but I had already disappeared. He had seen his father, instead, and this had enraged him. No, I couldn't understand. He was risking present and future with the Vossi shop. Would I believe him if I told me that he didn't have a moment's respite? But his father didn't realize the economic and emotional investment he had made in that enterprise. No, he didn't realize it. He tormented him with continuous requests for money, threatened him night and day on the telephone, and annoyed the clients on purpose. On the other hand I shouldn't think that he was always the way I had seen him in the funicular. If necessary the old man knew how to behave, a real gentleman, so that women listened to him. Then, when he changed his tune, there was trouble. He was losing money because of his father, but what could he do? Murder him?

I said to him dully: yes, of course, no, really. I was uneasy. My dress was soaked. I had glimpsed myself in the rearview mirror of the taxi and realized that the rain had dissolved the mask of makeup. My skin was like a grainy and faded fabric, striped by blue-black rivulets of mascara. I was cold. I would have preferred to return to my uncle's house, find out what had happened to him, reassure myself, take a hot bath, lie down. But that massive body beside me, bursting with food, with drink, with worries and resentment, who carried deep within himself a child smelling of cloves, of *millefiori* liqueur, and of nutmeg, with whom I had played secretly as a child, interested me more than the words he was saying. I assumed that he couldn't tell me things that I hadn't already told myself. I didn't count on that. But to see those enormous hands, broad and thick, and recall those of Antonio the child, and to feel that they were the same even though they displayed no sign of that time, kept me even from asking where we were going. Beside him I felt miniaturized, with a look and a size that I hadn't had for years. I skirted the painted desert of the counter of the *bar-coloniali*, I pushed aside a black curtain and entered another place, where Polledro's words couldn't penetrate. Here was his grandfather, Caserta's father, who was the color of bronze, bald, his skull dark, eyes whose whites were red, a long face, an almost toothless mouth. Various mysterious machines were ranged around him. One, which was sky-blue, and elongated, with a shiny bar across it, was used for making *gelati*. Another consisted of a bowl with a rotating mechanical arm, in which he whipped yellow cream. In the back there was an electric oven with three compartments, the peepholes dark when it was turned off, the handles black. And behind a marble counter Antonio's grandfather, grim and wordless, skillfully squeezed a cloth funnel from whose serrated mouth cream emerged. The cream extended over pastries and cakes in a beautiful wavy line. He ignored me as he worked. I felt pleasantly invisible. I stuck a finger in the bowl of cream, I ate a pastry, I took a candied fruit, stole some silver sugared almonds. He didn't bat an eyelid. Until Antonio appeared and gestured to me and opened, behind his grandfather, the door to the cellar. From there, from that place of spiders and mold, emerged, a hundred times in a row and in a few seconds, Caserta in a camelhair coat and Amalia in her dark suit, sometimes with hat and veil, sometimes without. I saw them and tried to close my eyes.

"My father has been well only in the last year," Polledro said in the tone of one who is preparing to exaggerate in order to take advantage of the benevolence of his listener. "Amalia showed toward him a gentleness, an understanding, that I would never have expected."

It was true—he went on, now changing his tone—that the old man had stolen a lot of money in order to dress fashionably and impress my mother. But Polledro wasn't complaining about that money. His father had gotten into something worse. And he was afraid that soon he would get himself into bigger trouble. No, it had been a real misfortune: Amalia shouldn't have done what she did. Drown herself. Why? What a shame, what a shame. Her death was a terrible thing.

At that point Polledro seemed overwhelmed by the memory of my mother and began to apologize for not coming to the funeral, for not having offered his condolences.

"She was an exceptional woman," he said again and again, even if they had probably never spoken to each other. And then he asked: "Did you know that she and my father were seeing each other?"

I said yes, looking out the window. They were seeing each other. And I saw myself on my mother's bed, as in astonishment I examined my vagina with a mirror. Seeing each other: Amalia had looked at me, uncertain, and then had slowly closed the bedroom door.

Now the taxi was hugging the gray and busy shoreline: the traffic was heavy and fast-moving, beaten by rain and wind. Tall waves rose from the sea. I had rarely as a girl seen such an impressive storm in the bay. It was like the naïve painted exaggerations of my father. The waves surged darkly, with white crests, easily overflowing the barrier of the rocks, sometimes coming up so far that they sprayed the pavement. The spectacle had attracted groups of the curious who, under forests of umbrellas, pointed with a shout to the highest crests as they hurtled in a million fragments over the seawall.

"Yes, I knew it," I repeated, with greater conviction.

He was silent for a moment, surprised. Then he began digressing about his own life: a harsh existence, his marriage in shreds, three children he hadn't seen for a year, difficulty of making a living. Only now was he climbing back up. And he was doing well. I? Was I married? Did I have children? Why not? Did I prefer to live free and independent? Lucky me. Now I would straighten myself up and we would have lunch together. He had to see some friends but, if I didn't mind, I could go with him. He didn't have time to spare, however, with a business it was like that. If I could be patient, then we could talk a little.

"Is that all right with you?" he finally remembered to ask.

I smiled, forgetting what I looked like, and followed him out of the taxi, blinded by the water and the wind, forced to move quickly by his hand that was holding me by the arm. He opened a door and pushed me through in front of him, like a hostage, without loosening his grip. I found myself in the lobby of a hotel of neglected splendor, of dusty and moth-eaten opulence. In spite of the precious wood and red velvet, the place seemed miserable: lights too dim for a gray day, an intense murmur of voices in dialect, the clatter of plates and silverware coming from a large room on my left, a strong odor of food, a rushing to and fro of waiters who exchanged rude remarks with each other.

"Is Moffa there?" Polledro asked in dialect of a man at the reception desk. He answered with a nod of irritation that meant: he certainly is, and he's been here for a while. Polledro left me and hurried to the entrance of the room, where a banquet was in progress. The man at the desk took advantage of this to give me a glance of disgust. I saw myself in a large tall mirror in a gilded frame. The light dress was pasted to my body. I seemed thinner and at the same time more muscular. My hair was stuck to my skull, so that it seemed painted on. My face was as if disfigured by an ugly skin disease, dark with mascara around the eyes and flaking or in patches on my cheekbones and cheeks. In one hand I carried the plastic bag in which I had put all the things I had found in my mother's suitcase.

Polledro returned, irritated. I understood that he was late because of his father and maybe because of me.

"What do I do now?" he asked the man at the desk.

"Sit, eat, and when the lunch is over talk to him."

"You can't find me a place at his table?"

"You're a fool," said the man. And he explained ironically, with the air of one who is saying something well known even to the most dull-witted, that at the table of that Moffa were professors, the rector, the mayor, the commissioner for culture, and their wives. A place at that table was unthinkable.

I looked at my childhood friend: he, too, was soaked and in disarray. I saw that he returned my look with embarrassment. He was agitated; the features of the child I remembered appeared and disappeared from his face. I felt pity for him and didn't want to. I moved toward the dining room to allow him to quarrel with the man at the desk without having to take account of my presence.

I leaned on the glass partition that looked onto the restaurant, careful not to get in the way of the waiters who were going in and out. The piercing voices and the rattle of silverware seemed to me of an insupportable volume. It was a sort of inaugural lunch, or maybe the conclusion, of some congress or convention. There were at least two hundred people. An evident disparity among the diners struck me. Some were restrained, intent, ill at ease, at times ironic, at times accommodating, in general soberly refined. Others were flushed, moving restlessly between food and talk, their bodies laden with everything that might signify the possibility of expense, of streams of money. It was particularly the women who synthesized the differences between their men. Slender bodies wrapped in clothing of a fine make, nourished with great frugality and discreetly illuminated by courteous smiles, sat beside bodies bursting out of tight dresses as costly as they were loud, sparkling with gold and jewels, peevishly silent or chattering and laughing.

From where I was it was difficult to calculate what advantages, what complicities, what ingenuities had brought people so visibly diverse to the same table. On the other hand it didn't interest me. It struck me only that the room seemed one of the places to which as a child I had imagined my mother escaping as soon as she left the house. If at that moment Amalia had entered, in her blue suit of decades earlier, the delicately colored scarf and the hat with the veil, on the arm of Caserta in his camelhair overcoat, she would certainly have crossed her legs ostentatiously, and looked happily, eyes shining, to right and to left. It was to feasts of food and laughter like this that I imagined her going when she left the house without me and I was sure she would never return. I pictured her brilliant with gold and silver, eating without restraint. I was sure that she, too, as soon as she left the house, stuck out a long red tongue. I wept in the storeroom, beside the bedroom.

"Now he'll give you the key," Polledro said speaking from behind me, without the kindness of before, in fact rudely. "Fix yourself up and join me at that table over there."

I saw him cross the room, skirting a long table, and addressing a deferential greeting to an old man who was speaking in a loud voice to a well-groomed, dignified woman with blue hair, arranged in an old-fashioned style. The greeting was ignored. Polledro looked away, furious, and went to sit down, with his back to me, at a table where a fat man with a black mustache and a heavily made-up woman, in a tight dress that rode too far above her knees when she sat, were devouring their food in silence, ill at ease.

I didn't like the way he had spoken to me. It was a tone of voice that gave orders and did not admit replies. I thought of crossing the room and telling my former playmate that I was leaving. But I was restrained by the way I knew I looked and by that formula: playmate. What sort of play? There had been games that I played with him only to see if I knew how to play as I imagined Amalia secretly did. All day my mother pedaled on her Singer like a cyclist in flight. At home she was modest and reserved, hiding her hair, her colored scarves, her dresses. But, just like my father, I suspected that outside the house she laughed differently, breathed differently, orchestrated the movements of her body in such a way as to make people stare. She turned the corner and went into the shop of Antonio's grandfather. She slipped around the bar, ate pastries and sugared almonds, meandered past counters, machines, and pans without getting dirty. Then Caserta arrived, and opened the iron door, and they went down together to the cellar. Here my mother loosened her long black hair and that abrupt movement filled the dark air smelling of earth and mold with sparks. Then they both lay down on the floor on their stomachs and crawled along, laughing. The cellar in fact extended as a long, low space. One could advance only on all fours, amid bits of wood and iron, crates and crates full of old tomato sauce jars, the breath of bats and the rustling of mice. Caserta and my mother crept along, keeping in sight the white squares of light that opened at fixed intervals on their left. They were vents, with nine bars across them and a fine-mesh screen to keep the mice from getting through. Children, on the outside, stared at the darkness and the wells of light, imprinting noses and foreheads with the grid pattern of the screen. They, on the other hand, looked out from the inside, to be sure of not being seen. Concealed in the darkest areas, they touched each other between the legs. Meanwhile I distracted myself, in order not to cry, and, since Antonio's grandfather did not make a move to hinder me but hoped to get revenge on Amalia by making me die of indigestion, stuffed myself with candies, with licorice, with cream scraped from the bottom of the bowl it was made in.

"208, on the second floor," an attendant said. I took the key and declined the elevator. I went slowly up a broad staircase, along which ran a red carpet, held in place by gilded rods.

17.

Room 208 was sordid, like a room in a third-rate hotel. It was at the end of a dimly lit dead-end corridor, next to a closet carelessly left open and full of brooms, carts, vacuum cleaners, dirty laundry. The walls were of a yellowish color and above the double bed was a Madonna of Pompeii; a dry olive branch had been inserted between the nail and the triangle of metal that held the image in the frame. The bathroom fixtures, which, given the pretensions of the hotel, should have been sealed, were dirty, as if they had just been used. The wastebasket hadn't been emptied. Between the bed and the wall was a narrow passage that allowed one to get to the window. I opened it, hoping that it would have a view onto the sea: naturally it faced an internal courtyard. I realized that it was no longer raining.

First I tried to telephone. I sat on the bed, avoiding looking at myself in the mirror opposite. I let the telephone ring for a long time, but Uncle Filippo didn't respond. Then I rummaged around in the plastic bag where I had stuck the things my mother had in her suitcase, and took out the bathrobe of ivory-colored satin and the short blue dress. The dress, thrown hastily into the bag, was all wrinkled. I laid it out on the bed, smoothing it with my hands. Then I took the bathrobe and went to the bathroom.

I undressed and took out the tampax: my period seemed to have abruptly ended. I wrapped the tampon in toilet paper and threw it in the wastebasket. I examined the base of the shower: disgusting short black hairs were scattered along the edges of the porcelain. I let the water run for a long time before getting under it. With satisfaction I realized that I could master the need to hurry. I was separated from myself: the woman who wanted to be shot off like an arrow, eyes wide open, was observed dispassionately by the woman under the water. I soaped myself carefully and did so in such a way that every gesture belonged to an external world without deadlines. I wasn't following anyone and no one was following me. I wasn't expected and I wasn't expecting visits. My sisters had left for good. My father was sitting in his old house before the easel and painting Gypsies. My mother, who for years had existed only as an annoying responsibility, at times nagging, was dead. But as I rubbed my face vigorously, especially around the eyes, I realized with unexpected tenderness that in fact I had Amalia under my skin, like a hot liquid that had been injected into me at some unknown time.

I wrung out my wet hair until it was almost dry, and looked closely in the mirror to make sure that no mascara remained on my eyelashes. I saw my mother just as she was represented on her identity card and smiled at her. Then I put on the satin robe, and for the first time in my life, in spite of the ugly ivory color, had the impression of being beautiful. I felt, for no apparent reason, the same pleasant surprise as when I found in unlikely places gifts that Amalia had hidden, pretending to have negligently forgotten dates and celebrations. She kept us in suspense until, suddenly, the gift appeared, in some everyday place that had nothing to do with its exceptional nature. Seeing us happy she was happier than we were.

I suddenly understood that the contents of the suitcase had been intended not for her but for me. The lie I had told the salesgirl at the Vossi sisters' shop was in fact the truth. Even the blue dress that waited for me on the bed was certainly my size. I realized it as if it were the robe itself on my skin telling me. I put my hands in the pockets, sure that I would find the birthday card. And in fact it was there, placed on purpose to surprise me. I opened the envelope and read Amalia's girlish writing, with the ornate letters that no one knows how to make anymore: "Happy birthday, Delia. Your mother." Immediately afterward I realized that my fingers were slightly sandy. I put my hands in the pockets and discovered that at the bottom was a thin layer of sand. My mother had worn that robe before drowning herself.

18.

I didn't notice that the door had opened. Instead I heard someone locking it. Polledro took off his jacket and threw it on a chair. He said in dialect:

"They won't give me a lira."

I looked at him in bewilderment. I didn't know what he was talking about: maybe a bank loan, maybe money at interest, maybe a bribe. He was like a weary husband who thought he could tell me his troubles as if I were his wife. With his jacket off, you could see the shirt swelling over the belt of his trousers, the chest and the large heavy breasts. I got ready to tell him to leave the room.

"Instead they want back the money they advanced." He continued his monologue from the bathroom and his voice reached me through the open door together with the flow of urine into the toilet. "My father asked Moffa for money without telling me. At his age, he wants to restore the old *pasticceria* on Via Gianturco and do with it who knows what. He told a pack of lies, as usual. So now Moffa won't trust me anymore. He says I don't know how to control the old man. They'll take away the shop."

"Weren't we supposed to have lunch together?" I asked.

He walked past me as if he hadn't heard. He went to the window and lowered the shade. The only light came faintly from the open door of the bathroom.

"You took your time," he reproached me, finally. "It means you'll skip lunch: at four the shop reopens, I don't have long."

I looked mechanically at the phosphorescent hands of the clock: it was ten of three.

"Let me get dressed," I said.

"You're fine like that," he said. "But be ready to give me back everything: dresses, robe, underpants."

I began to feel my heart pounding. I could hardly bear his dialect or the hostility he gave off. In addition I could no longer see the expression on his face, which kept me from gauging to what extent he was displaying an elementary model of virility, and to what extent, on the other hand, the model might materialize into real intentions of violence. I saw only the dark silhouette that was unknotting the tie.

"They are my things," I objected, pronouncing the words carefully. "My mother gave them to me for my birthday."

"They are things that my father took from the shop. So you have to give them back to me," he answered, with a slight childish dip in his voice.

I felt sure he wasn't lying. I imagined Caserta choosing those garments for me: colors, size, styles. I felt a shiver of disgust.

"I'll just take the dress and leave you all the rest," I said. So I reached my hand out toward the bed to grab the dress and slip into the bathroom, but the gesture sliced the air too quickly and hit the wall behind it, with the Madonna of Pompeii and the dry olive branch. I had to move more slowly. I brought my arm under control so that the whole room wouldn't become animated, with every object shifting, gripped by anxiety. I hated it when frenzy took charge.

Polledro noticed my hesitation and grabbed hold of my wrist. I didn't react, in order to keep him from trying to crush any hint of resistance by pulling me toward him. I knew I could keep at bay the impression of looming violence only if the speed of our movements seemed chosen by me.

He kissed me without embracing me, but keeping a strong grip on my wrist. First he pressed his lips against mine and then tried to open them with his tongue. He did it in such a way that I was reassured: yes, he was merely behaving as he thought a man should behave in those circumstances, but without real aggression, and perhaps without conviction. He had probably lowered the blind in order to take advantage of the darkness and surreptitiously change his appearance, relax the muscles of his face.

I half opened my lips. Forty years earlier I had imagined with fascinated horror that the little Antonio had the same tongue as Caserta, but I had never had proof of it. Antonio as a child had not been interested in kissing: he preferred to explore the entrance to my vagina with his dirty fingers and at the same time pull my hand toward his short pants. Then in time I had discovered that Caserta's tongue was a fantasy. None of the kisses I had had in my life seemed like the ones I had imagined him giving Amalia. And Antonio as an adult was confirming that he was not the equal of those fantasies. He didn't kiss me with much conviction. As soon as he realized that I had agreed to open my mouth, he pushed his tongue too impetuously between my teeth, and immediately, continuing to hold onto my wrist, pulled my hand over his pants. I felt that I shouldn't have opened my lips.

"Why in the dark?" I asked him in a low voice, with my mouth against his. I wanted to hear him speak, to be definitively sure that he wouldn't try to hurt me. But he didn't answer. His breath was short, he kissed my cheek, he licked my neck. Meanwhile he didn't stop pressing my hand, palm spread, against the fabric of his pants. He was insistent, so that I would understand that I shouldn't be inert. I held his sex. Only then did he let go of my wrist and embrace me. He murmured something I didn't understand and leaned over to find my nipples, pushing my chest back, tasting with his mouth the satin fabric and wetting the robe with saliva.

I knew then that nothing new would happen. It was the start of a well-known rite that I had experienced often as a young woman, hoping that if I changed men frequently my body would eventually come up with the appropriate response. Instead it was always the same, identical to what I was now expressing. Polledro had opened the robe to suck my breasts and I began to feel a slight pleasure, not localized, as if warm water were running over my numbed body. Meanwhile, with one hand, careful not to disturb my hand that was holding his member under the fabric, he was caressing my sex too ardently, excited by the discovery that I wasn't wearing underpants. Still I felt nothing but that diffuse pleasure, enjoyable and yet not urgent.

For a long time I had been sure that I would never cross

that threshold. I had only to wait for him to ejaculate. On the other hand, as always, I felt no impulse to help him, in fact I barely moved. I knew intuitively that he expected me to undo his pants, take out his penis, not confine myself to holding it. I felt that he was agitating his pelvis in an attempt to transmit hesitant instructions. I was unable to respond. I was afraid that my already slow breathing would stop completely. And I was paralyzed by a growing embarrassment, because of the copious liquids spilling out of me.

Even when as a girl I had tried to masturbate this had happened. The pleasure spread warmly, without any crescendo, and immediately my skin began to get wet. However much I caressed myself, the only result was that the liquids of my body overflowed: my mouth, instead of getting dry, filled with a cold saliva; sweat ran down my forehead, my nose, my cheeks; my armpits became puddles; not an inch of skin remained dry; my sex got so wet that the fingers slipped over it without purchase, and I could no longer tell if I was really touching myself or only imagined that I was. The tension of my body wouldn't increase: I was left worn out and unsatisfied.

Of all this Polledro for the moment seemed unaware. He pushed me toward the bed, and, in order to keep us from falling together with the velocity caused by his weight, I sat down cautiously and then submissively stretched out. I saw his shadow hesitating, for a few seconds indecisive. Then he took off his shoes, his trousers, his underpants. He got on the bed and sat astride me, on his knees, resting lightly on my stomach, without putting his weight on me.

"So?" he murmured.

"Come on," I said, but didn't move. He groaned, his chest erect: he was hoping that finally his sex, large and thick in the shadowy light, would mingle its desires with those he attributed to mine. Since nothing happened, after a deep breath he reached out one hand and began rubbing me between the legs again. He must have thought that like that he would finally induce me to react: out of passion, out of maternal pity, the modality of the reaction didn't seem important to him; he was only looking for the stimulus that would excite me. But my compliance without participation began to disorient him. I thought, as always in those circumstances, that I should pretend a yearning and uncontrolled passion or push him away. But I didn't dare to do either one or the other: I was afraid I would throw up, because the result would be earthquake-like waves. I had only to wait. Besides, I could no longer feel his fingers: maybe he had withdrawn in disgust, maybe he was still touching me but I had lost every sensibility.

Disappointed, Polledro took my hands and brought them around his sex. At that point I realized that he would never enter me unless he was sure I wanted him to. I also noticed that his erection was beginning to recede, like a defective neon light. He realized it, too, and shifted forward so that his stomach came close to my mouth. I felt for him a vague sympathy, as if he really were the child Antonio I had known; and I wanted to tell him that but my voice wouldn't come out: he was rubbing slowly against my lips and I was afraid that any slight, even imperceptible movement of my mouth would be so uncontrollable that it would lacerate his sex.

"Why did you come to the shop?" he asked, annoyed, sliding back along my body, which was dripping with sweat. "I didn't come looking for you."

"I didn't even know who you were," I said.

"And all that nonsense? The dress, the underpants . . . what did you want?"

"I didn't come to see you," I said, but without aggression. "I just wanted to see your father. I wanted to know what had happened to my mother before she drowned."

I realized that he wasn't convinced and was trying to caress me again. I shook my head to let him understand: enough. He squatted over me for an instant. He pulled back abruptly with a gesture of repulsion as he felt me soaking wet.

"You're not well," he said uncertainly.

"I'm fine. But even if I were sick, it would be too late to cure me."

Polledro turned over beside me in resignation. I saw in the half light that he was drying his fingers, his face, his legs with the sheet; then he turned on the lamp on the night table.

"You look like a ghost," he said, gazing at me, without irony, and, with an edge of shirt that he was still wearing, began to dry my face.

"It's not your fault," I reassured him and asked him to turn out the light again. I didn't want to be seen and didn't want to see him. Thus, lost and desolate, he too closely resembled Caserta as I had imagined him or had actually seen him forty years earlier. The impression was so intense that I even thought of telling him right then, in the dark, what I saw crowding around his face, which was so different from the puffy and thuggish face he had showed me all morning. Speaking, I wished to eliminate both me and him, in that bed, different from the children of long ago. We had in common only the violence we had witnessed.

When my father found out that Amalia and Caserta were seeing each other secretly in the cellar—I thought of telling him slowly, gently—he wasted no time. First of all he chased Amalia along the corridor, down the stairs, through the street. I smelled on him the odor of oil paints, when he went by, and it seemed to me that he himself was brightly painted.

My mother fled under the railway bridge, slipped in a puddle, was caught, and punched, slapped, kicked in the side. Once he had punished her sufficiently, he brought her home bleeding. As soon as she tried to speak, he struck her again. I looked at her for a long time, bruised and dirty, and she looked at me for a long time, while my father explained the situation to Uncle Filippo. Amalia had a look of wonder: she stared at me and didn't understand. Then, irritated, I went off to spy on the other two.

My father and Uncle Filippo had gone into the courtyard together and I could see them from the window: they were tin soldiers making serious decisions. Or officers to cut out and paste in an album, one beside the other so that they could speak privately. My father wore boots and had put on a bush jacket. Uncle Filippo was wearing an olive-green uniform, or maybe white, or black. Not only that: he had a gun.

Or he stayed in his regular clothes, even though in the shadowy light of room 208 a voice was still saying: "He'll kill him, he took the gun." Maybe it was those sounds which made me see my father in his boots, Uncle Filippo in uniform, with both arms hanging beside his chest and the gun in his right hand. Together they chased the young Caserta, in his camelhair coat, up the stairs to his house. Behind them, at a distance, so that she wouldn't be beaten again, or because she was worn out and couldn't run, there was Amalia in her blue suit and the hat with the feathers, who was saying in a low voice, more and more bewildered: "Don't kill him, he hasn't done anything."

Caserta lived on the top floor but first they caught him on the third. The three men had stopped there, as if for a secret meeting. In fact they had produced in unison a tumult of insults in dialect, a long list of words ending in consonants, as if the final vowel had been thrown into an abyss and the rest of the word were whining mutely in displeasure.

When the list ended, Caserta had been pushed down the stairs and had rolled to the first floor. At the bottom of the stairs he got up and ran up again: who could say whether to boldly confront the avengers or try to reach his house and his family on the fifth floor. The fact is that he got past them and— with one hand running lightly over the banister and then, when his body curved, grasping it, the legs continuously taking the steps three by three—whirled up the stairway to the door of his house, spurred by kicks that missed him and spit that sometimes struck him like a meteor.

My father got to him first and threw him to the floor. He pulled his head up by the hair and smashed it against the banister. The thuds were protracted into an interminable echo. Finally he left him unconscious, in the blood on the floor, on the advice of his brother-in-law, who may have had a gun but was wiser. Filippo took my father by one arm and dragged him away calmly: he did it because otherwise my father would have left Caserta dead on the floor. Caserta's wife, too, was pulling my father away: she was holding on to his other arm. Of Amalia there remained only her voice, which said: "Don't kill him, he hasn't done anything." Antonio, who had been my playmate, was crying but with his head down, suspended in the stairwell as if he were flying.

I heard Polledro breathing beside me in silence and felt compassion for the child he had been. "I'm going," I said.

I got up and put on the blue dress quickly to avoid his gaze on my shadow. I felt that the dress fit me perfectly. Then I looked in the plastic bag for a pair of white briefs and put them on, sliding them under the dress. I turned on the light. Polledro had an absent expression. I saw him and no longer could think that he had been Antonio, who resembled Caserta. His heavy body was lying on the bed, naked from the waist down. It was that of a stranger, without obvious connection to my past life or to the present, apart from the wet imprint I had left on his side. But at the same time I was grateful for the small dose of humiliation and pain he had inflicted on me. I went around the bed, sat on the edge beside him, and masturbated him. He let me do it, with his eyes closed. He ejaculated without a moan, as if he were feeling no pleasure.

19.

The sea had become a violet paste. The noise of the storm and the noise of the city made a furious commotion. I crossed the street, avoiding cars and puddles. More or less unharmed, I stopped to look at the façades of the great hotels lined up beside the fierce flow of vehicles. Every opening in those structures was spitefully shut against the din of the traffic and the sea.

I took the bus to Piazza Plebiscito. After a pilgrimage through damaged phone booths and bars with broken equipment, I finally found a telephone and dialed Uncle Filippo's number. There was no answer. I set off on Via Toledo as the shops were pulling up their shutters, the swarm of pedestrians already dense. People stood in little groups at the entrances to the alleys, steep and black under strips of dark sky. Near Piazza Dante I bought some chocolate, just to breathe the sweet air of the shop. In fact I had no wish for anything: I was so distracted that I forgot to put the chocolate in my mouth and it melted in my fingers. I paid little attention to the insistent looks of men.

It was hot, and in Port'Alba there was neither air nor light. Near my mother's house I was attracted by some fat, shiny cherries. I bought half a kilo, got on the elevator with no feeling of pleasure and went to knock on the door of the widow De Riso.

The woman opened it in her usual circumspect manner. I showed her the cherries, saying I had bought them for her. She widened her eyes. She released the door from the chain and invited me in, visibly pleased by that gift of unhoped-for sociability.

"No," I said, "come to my house. I'm waiting for a phone call." Then I added something about ghosts: I was certain—I assured her—that after a few hours they became less and less autonomous. "After a while they start doing and saying only what we order them to do. If we want them to be silent, finally they are silent."

My proper Italian made Signora De Riso uneasy. To accept the invitation she tried for a formality equal to mine; then she locked the door of her apartment while I opened the door of my mother's.

It was suffocating inside. I hurried to open the windows and put the cherries in a plastic container. I let the water run, while the old woman, after a suspicious look all around, sat down almost automatically at the kitchen table. She said, in explanation, that my mother always invited her in there.

I put the cherries down in front of her. She waited for me to ask her to take some, and, when I did, brought one to her mouth with a pleasing, childish gesture that I liked: she took it by the stalk and let it go in her mouth, rotating the fruit between tongue and palate without biting it, the green stalk dancing along her pale lips; then she grabbed the stem again with her fingers and pulled it off with a faint *plop*.

"Very good," she said and, relaxing, began to praise the dress I was wearing. Then she added emphatically: "I said that this blue would be better for you than the other."

I looked at the dress and then at her to be sure that she was referring to that dress. She had no doubts, she continued: it was very becoming. When Amalia had showed her the gifts for my birthday, she had immediately felt that that was the right dress for me. My mother, too, seemed certain. Signora De Riso told me that she was euphoric. There in the kitchen, at that very table, she had laid out the lingerie, the dresses, repeating, "They will look very good on her." And she was very pleased with how she had got them.

"How?" I asked.

"That friend of hers," said the widow De Riso. He had proposed an exchange: he wanted all her old lingerie in exchange for those new things. It cost him almost nothing, the swap. He was the proprietor of a very expensive shop on the Vomero. Amalia, who had known him since her youth and knew that he was very smart in business matters, suspected that he wanted to take those old underpants and mended slips as a starting point for some sort of new merchandise. But Signora De Riso was experienced in the world. She had said that, gentleman or not, old or young, rich or poor, with men it was always best to be wary. My mother was too happy to pay attention to her.

Noticing her deliberately equivocal tone, I felt like laughing but contained myself. I saw Caserta and Amalia, who, starting with her ancient rags, planned in that house together, night after night, a grand reintroduction of women's lingerie of the fifties. I invented a persuasive Caserta, a suggestible Amalia, old and alone, both without any money, in that squalid kitchen, a few feet from the sharp ears of the widow, just as old, just as alone. The scene seemed to me plausible. But I said:

"Maybe it wasn't a real exchange. Maybe her friend wanted to do her a favor and that was all. Don't you think?"

The widow ate another cherry. She didn't know what to do with the pits: she spit them into the palm of her hand and left them there.

"Maybe," she admitted, but dubiously. "He was very respectable. He came almost every night and sometimes they dined together, sometimes they went to the cinema, sometimes for a walk. When I heard them on the landing, he was talking nonstop and your mother was always laughing."

"There's nothing wrong with that. It's nice to laugh."

The old woman hesitated as she chewed her cherries.

"Your father had made me suspicious," she said.

"My father?"

My father. I suppressed the sensation that he was already there, in the kitchen, and had been for a long time. Signora De Riso explained that he had come secretly to ask her to warn him if she noticed Amalia doing reckless things. It wasn't the first time he had appeared suddenly with requests of that sort. But on this occasion he had been very insistent.

I wondered what, for my father, the difference was between something that was reckless and something that wasn't. Signora De Riso seemed to realize this and in her way tried to explain it to me. Reckless was to carelessly expose oneself to the risks of existence. My father worried about his wife, even though they had been separated for twenty-three years. The poor man still loved her. He was so kind, so . . . Signora De Riso searched carefully for the right Italian word. She said: "desolate."

I knew it. He had tried as usual to make a good impression on the widow. He had been affectionate, he had said he was worried. But in fact—I thought—there was no barrier of the city that could keep him from hearing the echo of Amalia's laugh. My father couldn't bear her laugh. He thought that her laugh had a recycled, patently false resonance. Whenever there was a stranger in the house (for example the men who appeared at certain intervals to commission street urchins, Gypsies, or the classic Vesuvio with pine tree), he warned her: "Don't laugh." That laugh seemed to him added on purpose to humiliate him. In reality Amalia was only trying to give voices to the happy-looking women photographed or drawn on the posters and in the magazines of the forties: wide painted mouth, sparkling teeth, lively gaze. She imagined herself like that, and had found the appropriate laugh. It must have been difficult for her to choose the laugh, the voice, the gestures that her husband could tolerate. You never knew what was all right, what wasn't. Someone who passes on the street and looks at you. A joking remark. A careless nod. See, they rang at the door. See, they were delivering roses to her. See, she didn't reject them. She laughed instead, and chose a vase of blue glass, and arranged them in the container that she had filled with water. During the time when those mysterious gifts arrived regularly, those anonymous homages (but we all knew they were from Caserta: Amalia knew it), she had been young and seemed to be playing games with herself, without malice. She let the black curl fall over her forehead, she batted her eyelashes, she gave tips to the delivery boys, she allowed the things to remain in our house as if their remaining were permitted. Then my father would find out and destroy everything. He tried to destroy her, too, but he always managed to stop a step from stupidity. Yet the blood bore witness to the intention. While Signora De Riso was talking to me, I was telling myself about the blood. In the bathroom sink. It dripped from Amalia's nose, thick, without stopping, and first it was red, then, when it touched the water from the tap, faded. It was also on her arm, up to the elbow. She tried to stanch it with one hand but it flowed out from under the palm, leaving red lines like scratches. It wasn't innocent blood. To my father nothing about Amalia ever seemed innocent. He, so furious, so bitter and yet so eager for pleasure, so irascible and so egotistical, couldn't bear that she had a friendly, at times even joyful, relationship with the world. He recognized in it a trace of betrayal. Not only sexual betrayal: I no longer believed that he feared only being betrayed by sex. I was certain, rather, that above all he feared abandonment, passage into the enemy camp, acceptance of the rationales, the lexicon, the taste of people like Caserta: faithless intriguers, without rules, crude seducers to whom he had to bow out of necessity. So he tried to impose on her a code of behavior intended to communicate distance if not hostility. But soon he exploded in insults. Amalia's tone of voice, according to him, was too easily engaging; the gestures of her hands were too soft and slow; her gaze was eager to the point of shameless. Above all she could charm without effort and without the ambition to charm. It happened, even if she didn't intend it. Oh yes: for that, for her charm he punished her with slaps and punches. He interpreted her gestures, her looks, as signs of dark dealings, of secret meetings, of allusive understandings meant to marginalize him. I had trouble removing him from my vision, so anguished, so violent. The force. He petrified me. The image of my father as he ravaged the roses, stripping off the petals, shouted and shouted down the decades in my head. Now he was burning the new dress that she hadn't sent back, that she had worn in secret. I couldn't bear the odor of burned fabric. Even though I had opened the window.

"He came back and beat her?" I asked.

The woman admitted reluctantly:

"He showed up here early one morning, not later than six, and threatened to kill her. He said really terrible things to her."

"When was that?"

"Mid-May: a week before your mother left."

"And Amalia had already got the dresses and the new lingerie?"

"Yes."

"And she was pleased?"

"Yes."

"How did she react?"

"The way she always reacted. She forgot about it as soon as he left. I saw him go out: he was white as a fish in flour. She, on the other hand, nothing. She said: he's like that; not even old age has changed him. But I understood that things weren't completely clear. Until she left, until the train, I kept saying to her: Amalia, be careful. Nothing. She seemed tranquil. But on the way she had trouble keeping up her normal pace. She slowed down on purpose. In the compartment she started laughing for no reason and began to fan herself with a hem of her skirt."

"What's wrong with that?" I asked.

"It's not done," the widow answered.

I took two cherries with joined stems and hung them on my outstretched index finger, swinging them to the right and the left. Probably in the course of her existence Amalia had given up doing many things that, like every human being, she might legitimately or not legitimately have done. But perhaps she only pretended not to have done them. Or perhaps she had given the appearance of someone who pretends, so that my father would be constantly thinking of her unreliability and suffer for it. Perhaps that was her way of reacting. But she hadn't taken into account that we, her daughters, might think that, too, and forever: I above all. I couldn't remake her innocent. Not even now. It was possible that Caserta, looking for her companionship, had only been pursuing a fragment of his youth. But I was sure that Amalia was still playing the game with herself, opening the door with youthful mischief, pulling the curl over her eyebrows and batting her eyelashes. It was possible that with that nonsense of the businessman full of ideas the old man had only wanted to communicate his fetishism in a discreet way. But she hadn't pulled back. She had immediately laughed knowingly at the exchange, and had supported it with her own and his senile impulses, using me and my birthday. No, yes. I realized that I was summarizing a woman without prudence and without the virtue of fear. I had memories of it. Even when my father raised his fists and struck her, to shape her like a stone or a log, she widened her eyes not in fear but in astonishment. She must have widened her eyes in the same way when Caserta proposed the exchange. With joyful astonishment. I, too, was astonished, as if watching a scene of violence, a game for two created from conventions: the scarecrow that doesn't scare, the victim who isn't annihilated. It occurred to me that ever since she was a girl Amalia had thought of hands as gloves, silhouettes first of paper, then of leather. She had sewed and sewed. Then, moving on, she had reduced widows of generals, wives of dentists, sisters of magistrates to measurements of bust and hips. Those measurements, taken by discreetly embracing, with her seamstress's tape, female bodies of all ages, became paper patterns that, fastened to the fabric with pins, portrayed on it the shadows of breasts and hips. Now, intently, she cut the material, stretched tight, following the outline imposed by the pattern. For all the days of her life she had reduced the uneasiness of bodies to paper and fabric, and perhaps it had become a habit, and so, out of habit, she tacitly rethought what was out of proportion, giving it the proper measure. I had never thought about this, and now that I had I couldn't ask her if it really had been like that. Everything was lost. But, in front of Signora De Riso as she ate cherries, I found that that final game of fabrics between her and Caserta, that reduction of their underground history to a conventional exchange of old garments for new, was a sort of ironic fulfillment. My mood abruptly changed. I was suddenly content to believe that her carelessness had been thought out. Unexpectedly, surprisingly, I liked that woman who in some way had completely invented her story, playing on her own with empty fabrics. I imagined that she hadn't died unsatisfied, and I sighed with unexpected satisfaction. I took the cherries that I had been playing with and hung them over one ear. I laughed.

"How do I look?" I asked the old woman, who meanwhile had piled up in her cupped palm at least ten pits.

She scowled uncertainly.

"Good," she said, without conviction.

"I know," I declared, with, instead, an air of satisfaction. And I chose two more cherries with joined stems. I was about to put them on my other ear, but I changed my mind and held them out to Signora De Riso.

"No," she defended herself, drawing back.

I got up, walked behind her, and, as she shook her head, laughing nervously, flushed, freed her right ear from the gray hair and placed the cherries on the auricle. Then I stood back to admire the sight.

"Beautiful!" I exclaimed.

"No," the widow murmured, embarrassed.

I chose another pair of cherries and went back behind her to adorn the other ear. Afterward I embraced her, crossing her arms over her large bosom and hugging her hard.

"*Mammina*," I said to her. "It was you who told my father everything, isn't that true?"

Then I kissed her wrinkled neck, which was rapidly turning red. She squirmed in my arms, whether from uneasiness or the wish to free herself, I don't know. She denied it, said that she would never do that: how could that occur to me?

She had, however, done it—I thought. She had played the spy, in order to hear him shout, slam doors, break dishes, enjoying it anxiously from within the nest of her apartment.

The telephone rang. I kissed her again, hard, on her gray head, before going to answer: it was already the third ring.

"Hello," I said.

Silence.

"Hello," I repeated, calmly, as I observed Signora De Riso staring at me hesitantly and meanwhile struggling to get up from her chair.

I hung up.

"Please, stay a little longer," I invited her, becoming formal again. "Would you like to give me the pits? Eat the rest of the cherries. Just one more. Or take them with you."

But I felt that my tone was not reassuring. The old woman was standing now and was heading toward the door, with the cherries astride her ears.

"Are you angry with me?" I asked her, in a placating voice.

She looked at me in amazement. She must suddenly have thought of something that stopped her in her tracks.

"That dress," she said to me, in bewilderment, "how did you get it? You shouldn't have. It was in the suitcase with the other things. And the suitcase was never found. Where did you get it? Who gave it to you?"

As she spoke, I saw that her pupils were switching rapidly from astonishment to fear. I wasn't happy about that, I hadn't intended to frighten her, I didn't like causing alarm. I smoothed the dress with the palms of my hands as if to make myself taller; constricted by that short, close-fitting dress, too stylish, unsuitable for my age, I felt apprehensive.

"It's only fabric without memory," I murmured. I meant that it could do no harm to either me or her. But the widow De Riso hissed:

"It's dirty."

She opened the door and closed it behind her quickly. Just then the telephone rang again.

20.

I let it ring two or three times. Then I lifted the receiver: buzzing, distant voices, indecipherable sounds. I repeated "hello" without hope, just so that Caserta would know that I was there, that I wasn't frightened. Finally I hung up. I sat down at the kitchen table, took the cherries off my ear, and ate them. By now I knew that all the calls that followed would have the pure function of a reminder, a sort of whistle like the one that in the past men used when they wanted to announce from the street that they were coming home and the women could put the pasta on.

I checked the clock: it was ten after six. To keep Caserta from forcing me again to listen to his silence, I picked up the receiver and dialed Uncle Filippo's number. I was prepared for the long sound of the rings. Instead he answered, but without enthusiasm, as if annoyed by the fact that it was me. He said that he had just come in, that he was tired and cold, that he wanted to go to bed. He coughed artificially. He mentioned Caserta only when I asked, and then was irritated. He said they had talked for a long time but without quarreling. They had suddenly realized that there was no longer any reason for it. Amalia was dead, life had moved on.

He was silent for a moment, to let me speak: he expected some reaction. I had none. So he started muttering about old age, about solitude. He said that Caserta had been thrown out of the house by his son, had been left on his own, just like that, without a roof, worse than a dog. First the boy had stolen all the money he had saved and then had thrown him out. His only good fortune had been Amalia's kindness. Caserta had confided to him that they had seen each other again after many years: she had helped him, they had kept each other company, but discreetly, with mutual respect. Now he lived like a tramp, a little here, a little there. These were things that not even someone like him deserved.

"A fine man," I commented.

Filippo became even colder.

"There comes a time when one has to make peace with one's neighbor."

"And the girl on the funicular?" I asked.

My uncle was embarrassed.

"Sometimes it happens," he said. I didn't know it yet but I, too, would find out that old age is a brute, ferocious beast. Then he added: "There's worse foolishness than that." Finally he said, with uncontrolled bitterness:

"Between him and Amalia there was never anything."

"Maybe it's true," I admitted.

He raised his voice.

"Then why did you tell us those things?"

I retorted:

"Why did you believe me?"

"You were five years old."

"Exactly."

My Uncle Filippo sniffed. He murmured:

"Go away. Forget it."

"Take care of yourself," I advised him and hung up.

I stared at the telephone for a few seconds. I knew that it would ring: somewhere Caserta was waiting for the line to be free. The first ring was not long in coming. I made up my mind and left quickly, without locking the door.

There were no more clouds, there was no more wind. A whitish light reduced the Arciconfraternita di Santa Maria delle Grazie, tiny between the transparent façades of ordinary buildings covered with advertisements. I headed toward the taxis, then changed my mind and went into the yellow building where the subway entrance was. The crowd rustled beside me as if it were made of paper cutouts intended to amuse children. The sound of obscenities uttered in dialect—the only obscenities that could fit together sound and sense in my head in such a way as to make concrete a sex that was troublesome in its aggressive, pleasure-seeking, and sticky realism: every other formula outside of that dialect seemed to me insignificant, often lighthearted, pronounceable without repulsion—softened in an unexpected way, becoming a kind of rustling against the roller of an old typewriter. As I descended into the underground at Piazza Cavour, a warm wind blew in, making the metallic walls sway and mixing the red and blue of the escalator, and I imagined I was a figure from Neapolitan cards: the eight of spades, the woman who, calm and armed, advances on foot ready to jump into the game of *briscola*. I bit my lips between my teeth until they hurt.

The whole way I kept looking behind me. I couldn't see Caserta. To get a better view of the half-empty areas of the platform between the two black holes of the tunnel, I mingled where the crowd of waiting passengers was thickest. The train was full but emptied out soon afterward, in the neon half-light of the station at Piazza Garibaldi. I got out at the end of the line and, after a short set of steps, found myself beside the old cigarette factory, on the edge of the neighborhood where I had grown up.

The rural feeling it had had, with its four-story white buildings constructed in the middle of the dusty countryside, had been transformed over the years, and it had become a jaundiced neighborhood of the periphery, dominated by skyscrapers, choked by traffic and by the trains that, slowing down, snaked alongside the buildings. I turned immediately to the left, toward an overpass with three tunnels that went under it, the middle one closed by reconstruction work. I recalled a single endless passage, deserted and constantly shaken by the trains on the siding overhead. Instead I took no more than a hundred steps, slowly, in a shadowy light stinking of urine, squeezed between a wall that sweated large drops of water and a dusty guardrail that protected me from the crowded automobile lane.

The overpass had been there since Amalia was sixteen. She had had to walk through those cool shady tunnels when she went to deliver the gloves. I had always imagined that she carried them into the space I was leaving behind me, to an old factory with a tile roof that now displayed a Peugeot sign. But surely it wasn't like that. But what was like that? There was no longer any gesture or step there that, though the stones and the shadows were the same, could help me. Amalia had been followed in the tunnel by peddlers, railway workers, idlers, stonemasons chewing on rolls stuffed with broccoli and sausage or drinking wine from flasks. She told us, when she felt like telling us, that they stayed close, at her side, often breathing in her ear. They tried to touch her hair, her shoulder, her arm. Some tried to take her hand while making obscene remarks. She kept her eyes down and walked faster. Sometimes she burst out laughing, unable to contain herself. Then she would start running faster than her pursuer. How she ran: as if she were playing. She ran in my head. Was it possible that I, passing through there, carried her in my aging, unsuitably dressed body? Was it possible that her sixteen-year-old body, in a homemade flowered dress, was passing through the shadowy light by means of mine, nimbly avoiding the puddles, as she hurried toward the arc of yellow light that contained the anachronism of a Mobil gas pump?

Maybe, in the end, all that mattered of these two days without respite was the transplanting of the story from one head to the other, like a healthy organ that my mother had given up to me out of affection. My father, too, barely twenty, had chased her on that stretch of road. Amalia told us that, hearing him behind her, she was frightened. He wasn't like the others, who talked about her, trying to win her over. He talked about himself: he boasted of the extraordinary things he was capable of: he said he wanted to make a portrait of her, perhaps to prove to her how beautiful she was and how talented he was. He alluded to the colors she wore. How many words vanished who could say where. My mother, who never looked any of her pursuers in the face and while they talked made an effort not to laugh, told us that she had glanced at him sideways just once and had immediately understood. We, her daughters, did not understand. We couldn't understand why she liked him. Our father did not appear to us at all exceptional, slovenly as he was, fat, bald, unwashed, his sagging pants smeared with paint, always grumbling about the miseries of every day, about the money that he earned and that—he yelled at us—Amalia threw out the window. Yet it was that man without a job whom our mother had asked to come to her house if he wanted to talk to her: she wouldn't make love in secret; she had never done so. And when she uttered the words "make love" I listened open-mouthed, I liked the story of that moment so much, without its sequel, stopped before it could continue and be ruined. I preserved the sounds and images. Maybe now I had come to that underpass so that the sounds and images would coalesce again among the rocks and shadows, and again my mother, before she became my mother, was followed by the man with whom she would make love, who would cover her with his name, who would annihilate her with his alphabet.

I walked faster, after making sure yet again that Caserta hadn't followed me. The neighborhood, in spite of the disappearance of a number of details (on the yellow-green pond where I used to play an eight-story building had risen), seemed to me still recognizable. Children shouted in the potholed streets as they always had at the start of summer. The same cries in dialect came from the houses, with their open windows. The layout of the buildings followed the same unimaginative geometry. Even some impoverished commercial enterprises of that time had lasted over the decades: for example, the shop underground, where I had gone to buy soap and lye for my mother, was still open in the same crumbling structure of so many years earlier. Now it displayed on the threshold brooms of every type, plastic containers, and drums of detergent. I looked in for a moment, thinking I would find there the broad cavern of my memory. Instead it closed on me like a broken umbrella.

The building where my father lived was a few meters away. I had been born in that house. I went through the gate and made my way securely among the low, poor structures. I entered through a dusty doorway: the tiles of the entrance were broken, there was no elevator, the marble of the stairs was cracked and yellowed. The apartment was on the third floor and I hadn't been there for about ten years. As I went up I tried to redraw the map of it in such a way that the impact with that space wouldn't be too disturbing. The door opened onto a corridor without windows. There were two rooms and a kitchen. At the back on the left was the dining room, irregularly shaped, with a silverware cupboard for silverware that we had never had, a table used for some festive lunches, and a double bed where I and my sisters slept, after nightly quarrels to decide who of the three was to sacrifice and sleep in the middle. Next to that was the toilet, a long room with a narrow window, containing the toilet and a movable bidet of enameled metal. After that came the kitchen: the sink where in the morning we took turns washing, a hearth of white majolica that had fallen quickly into disuse, a copper boiler full of pots that Amalia polished carefully. Finally there was my parents' bedroom, and, next to it, a storeroom with no light, suffocating, crammed with useless objects.

We were forbidden to enter my father and mother's room: it was tiny. Opposite the bed was an armoire with a mirrored central panel. On the right-hand wall was a dressing table with a rectangular mirror. On the opposite side, between the edge of the bed and the window, my father had set up the easel, a tall, massive object, with thick feet, gnawed by woodworms, from which hung dirty rags for drying the brushes. A few inches from the edge of the bed was a chest where the tubes of paint were thrown randomly: the white was the biggest and the most easily identifiable, even when it had been squeezed and rolled up to the threaded neck; but many of the tubes were remarkable, sometimes for a name that recalled the prince in a fairy tale, like Prussian blue, sometimes for the aura of devastating fire, like burnt sienna. The cover of the chest was of plywood, and movable, and on it stood a carafe that held brushes and another that held turpentine, and a gulf of colors mixed by the brushes in a many-colored sea. The octagonal tiles of the floor there had disappeared under a gray crust that had dripped down from the brushes over the years. There were rolls of prepared canvases, provided by the men who commissioned the work; the same who later, having given him a few lire, took care of delivering the finished product to the traveling peddlers, offering their wares on the city sidewalks, in the neighborhood markets, at village fairs. The house was pervaded by the odor of oil paints and turpentine but none of us noticed it any longer. Amalia had slept with my father for almost two decades without ever complaining.

On the other hand she did complain when he stopped making portraits of women for the American sailors and scenes of the bay and began to work on the half-naked dancing Gypsy. I had only a confused memory of that time, based more on Amalia's stories than on direct experience: I was no more than four. The bedroom walls were crowded with exotic women in bright colors, interspersed with sketches of nudes drawn with a blood-red pastel. Often the poses of the Gypsy were rough copies of some photographs of women that my father kept hidden in a box in the closet and that I peeked at in secret. At other times the shapes of the blood-red nudes appeared in oil paintings.

I had no doubt that the pastel sketches reproduced my mother's body. I imagined that at night, when they closed the door of their bedroom, Amalia took off her clothes, posed like the naked women in the photographs in the closet, and said: "Draw." He took a roll of yellow paper, tore off a piece, and drew. What he did best was the hair. He would leave those women without features but above the empty oval of the face he would skillfully draw a majestic construction, unmistakably similar to the beautiful creation that Amalia knew how to make with her long hair. I tossed and turned in the bed, unable to sleep.

When our father finished the Gypsy, I was sure of it and so was Amalia: the Gypsy was her: less beautiful, the proportions wrong, the colors smudged; but her. Caserta saw it and said it was no good, it wouldn't sell. He seemed annoyed. Amalia intervened, she said she agreed. She and Caserta teamed up against my father. There was a discussion. I heard their voices streaming down the stairs. When Caserta left, my father without warning hit Amalia twice in the face with his right hand, first with the palm and then the back. I remembered that gesture precisely, with its wavelike motion, going and coming: I was seeing it for the first time. She fled to the end of the hall, to the storeroom, and tried to lock herself in. She was dragged out and kicked. One blow struck her in the hip and hurled her against the armoire in the bedroom. Amalia got up and tore all the drawings off the walls. He caught her, grabbed her by the hair, pounded her head against the mirror of the armoire, which broke.

People liked the Gypsy, especially at the country fairs. Forty years had passed and my father was still doing it. In time he had become very quick. He attached the blank canvas to the easel and sketched the outlines with an expert hand. Then the body became bronze with reddish highlights. The belly curved, the breasts swelled, the nipples rose. Meanwhile sparkling eyes emerged, red lips, raven hair, masses of it, combed in Amalia's style, which over time had become old-fashioned but evocative. In a few hours the canvas was finished. He took out the thumbtacks that held it in place, pinned it to the wall to dry, and arranged another blank canvas on the easel. Then he began again.

During adolescence I saw those figures of a woman leave the house in the hands of strangers who were not sparing with their crude comments. I didn't understand and perhaps there was nothing to understand. How was it possible that my father could hand over, to vulgar men, bold and seductive versions of that body which if necessary he would defend with a murderous rage? How could he place it in lewd poses when for an immodest smile or look he became a wild beast, without pity? Why did he abandon it on the streets and in the houses of strangers, by the tens and hundreds of copies, when he was so jealous of the original? I looked at Amalia bent over her sewing machine until late at night. I thought that, as she worked like that, silent and preoccupied, she, too, asked herself those questions.

21.

The door of the apartment was half-open. I felt timid and so I entered with such determination that the door hit the wall with a crash. There was no reaction. Only an intense odor of paint and cigarette smoke hit me. I went into the bedroom with the sensation that over the years the rest of the apartment had fallen apart. I was certain, however, that in that room everything remained unchanged: the double bed, the armoire, the dressing table with the rectangular mirror, the easel beside the window, the canvases rolled up in every corner, the stormy seas, the Gypsies, and the country idylls. My father's back was to me, large and bent, in an undershirt. His sharp skull was bald, spotted with dark patches. A shock of white hair covered his neck.

I moved slightly to the right in order to see in the proper light the canvas he was working on. He was painting with his mouth open, glasses on the tip of his nose. In his right hand was the brush that, after touching down among the paints, moved securely over the canvas; between the index and middle fingers of his left hand was a lighted cigarette, half of it ash about to fall to the floor. After a few brushstrokes he drew back and stood motionless for a few seconds; then he emitted a sort of "ah," a light, sonorous sigh, and began mixing colors again, inhaling on his cigarette. The painting wasn't at a good point: the bay stagnated in a blue stain; Vesuvius, farther along, sat under a fiery red sky.

"The sea can't be blue if the sky is that red," I said.

My father turned and looked at me above his glasses.

"Who are you?" he asked in dialect, hostile in both expression and tone. He had big purple bags under his eyes. The most recent memory I had of him struggled to coincide with that yellowish face, drowning in undigested emotions.

"Delia," I said.

He stuck the brush in one of the carafes. He got up from the chair with a long guttural groan and turned toward me, legs spread, back bent, rubbing his paint-stained hands on his sagging pants. He looked at me with growing perplexity. Then he said, in sincere astonishment:

"You've gotten old."

I realized that he didn't know whether to embrace me, kiss me, ask me to sit down, or start shouting and chase me out of the house. He was surprised but not pleasantly: he felt me as a presence out of place, perhaps he wasn't even certain that I was his oldest daughter. The rare times we had seen each other, after his separation from Amalia, we had quarreled. In his head the real daughter should have been trapped in a petrified adolescence, mute and accommodating.

"I'll leave right away," I reassured him. "I just came by to find out about my mother."

"She's dead," he said. "I was thinking about how she died before me."

"She killed herself," I said very clearly, but without emphasis.

My father grimaced and I realized that he was missing his upper incisors. The lower ones had become long and yellow.

"She went swimming at Spaccavento," he muttered, "at night, like a girl."

"Why didn't you come to the funeral?"

"When you're dead you're dead."

"You should have come."

"Will you come to mine?"

I thought for a moment and answered:

"No."

The big bags under his eyes darkened.

"You won't come because I'll die after you," he muttered. Then, unexpectedly, he punched me.

His fist hit me in the right shoulder and I had trouble controlling the part of me that was annihilated by that gesture.

The physical pain, on the other hand, seemed to me a small thing.

"You're a whore, like your mother," he said, his breath coming hard, and meanwhile he grabbed the chair in order not to fall. "You left me here like an animal."

I sought my voice in my throat and only when I was sure of it did I answer him:

"Why did you go to her house? You tortured her up until the end."

He tried to hit me again, but this time I was prepared: he missed and became more enraged.

"What did she think about me?" he began to shout. "I never knew what she thought. She was a liar. You were all liars."

"Why did you go to her house?" I repeated calmly.

He said:

"To kill her. Because she thought she could enjoy her old age, leaving me to rot in this room. Look what I have under here. Look."

He raised his right arm and showed me his armpit. He had some purplish pustules among the hairs curly with sweat.

"You won't die from that," I said.

He lowered his arm, exhausted by the tension. He tried to straighten his trunk but his spine wouldn't move more than an inch or so. He remained with his legs planted, one hand wrapped around the chair, a hoarse whisper coming from his chest. Maybe he, too, thought that in the world at that moment there remained only that floor, only the chair he was holding onto.

"I followed them for a week," he murmured. "He came every night at six, well dressed, jacket and tie: like a fashion plate. Half an hour later they went out. She wore her usual old things but she arranged them in a way that made her seem young. Your mother was a lying woman, with no sense. She walked beside him and they talked. Then they went to a restaurant or a film. They walked arm in arm and she acted the way she did whenever there was a man: the voice so, the hand so, the head, the hips."

As he talked he waved one flabby hand around his chest, shook his head and batted his eyelashes, stuck out his lips, wiggled his hips contemptuously. He was changing his strategy. First he wanted to frighten me, now he wanted to amuse me by mocking Amalia. But he possessed nothing of her, of any of the Amalias we had invented for ourselves, not even the worst. And he was not amusing. He was just an old man deprived of any humanity by frustration and rage. Maybe he expected some complicity, a hint of a smile. I refused. Instead I concentrated all my energy on repressing disgust. He realized it and was embarrassed. He was facing the canvas he was working on and I suddenly realized that, with that fiery red sky, he was trying to paint an eruption.

"You humiliated her as usual," I said.

My father shook his head in confusion and sat down again with a long groan.

"I went to tell her that I didn't want to live alone anymore," he muttered and stared spitefully at the bed beside him.

"You wanted her to come back and live with you?"

He didn't answer. From the window came an orange light that beat against the glass, reflecting in the mirror of the armoire and spreading through the room, lighting up its disorder and squalor.

"I have a lot of money put aside," he said. "I told her: I have a lot of money."

He added some other things that I didn't hear. While he spoke, I saw obliquely, under the window, the table that I had admired as a girl in the window of the Vossi sisters' shop. The two shouting women whose profiles almost coincided—hurled from right to left in a mutilated movement of hands, feet, part of the head, as if the table had been unable to contain them or had been bluntly sawed off—had ended up there, in that room, among the stormy seas, the Gypsies, and the pastoral scenes. I let out a long sigh of exhaustion.

"Caserta gave you that," I said, pointing at the painting. And I realized that I had been wrong: it wasn't Signora De Riso who had told him about Caserta and Amalia. It was Caserta himself. He had come there, had given him something he had wanted for decades, had talked about himself, had told him that old age is brutal, that his son had thrown him out on the street, that between him and Amalia there had always been a devoted and respectful friendship. And he had believed him. And perhaps my father had told him about himself. And certainly they had found themselves desolate and companions in misery. I felt I was a thing, mysteriously balanced in the center of the room.

My father grew agitated in the chair.

"Amalia was a liar," he burst out. "She never told me that you hadn't seen or heard anything."

"You were dying to beat up Caserta. You wanted to get rid of him, you thought that with the Gypsies you would finally make some money. You suspected that Amalia liked him. When I came to tell you that I had seen them together in the basement of the candy store, you had already imagined more than what I was telling you. What I said served only to give you an excuse."

He stared at me in surprise.

"You remember that? I don't remember anything anymore."

"I remember everything or almost everything. Only the words are missing. But I remember the horror and I feel it again every time someone in this city opens his mouth."

"I thought you didn't remember," he muttered.

"I remembered but I couldn't tell myself."

"You were a small child. How could I imagine . . . "

"You could imagine. You were always able to imagine when it was a matter of hurting her. You went to Amalia to see her suffer. You told her it was Caserta who came to you on purpose to tell you about the two of them. You said that he had told you about me, about how I had lied, forty years ago. You unloaded all the blame on her. And you accused her of having made me a sick little liar."

My father tried again to get up from his chair.

"You were repulsive even as a child," he cried. "It was you who pushed your mother to leave me. You used me and then you threw me away."

"You ruined her life," I retorted. "You never helped her to be happy."

"Happy? I was never happy, either."

"I know."

"Caserta seemed better than me. You remember the gifts that came for her? She knew perfectly well that Caserta sent them in his own interest, to get revenge: today fruit; tomorrow a book; then a dress; then flowers. She knew that he did it so that I would be suspicious of her and kill her. It would have been enough if she had refused those gifts. But she didn't. She took the flowers and put them in a vase. She read the book without even hiding it. She put on the dress and went out. Then she let herself be hit till she was bleeding. I couldn't trust her. I couldn't understand what she was hiding in her head. I couldn't understand what she was thinking."

Pointing to the table behind him, I murmured:

"You aren't able to resist Caserta's gifts, either."

He turned to look at the painting, uneasily.

"I did it," he said. "It's not a gift. It's mine."

"You wouldn't be capable of that," I said.

"I did it as a young man," he insisted, and I had the impression that he was imploring me to believe him. "I sold it to the Vossi sisters in 1948."

I sat on the bed without his asking me, next to his chair. I said to him gently:

"I'm going."

He started.

"Wait."

"No," I said.

"I won't bother you. We can get along together. What kind of work do you do?"

"I draw comic strips."

"Does it pay well?"

"I don't have many needs."

"I've got money put aside," he repeated.

"I'm used to living frugally," I said. And I thought of chasing him out of the childhood part of my memory by embracing him, here, now, to make him human, as perhaps he was, in reality, in spite of everything. I didn't have time. He struck me again, in the chest. I pretended not to feel any pain. I pushed him back, I got up and went out without even glancing at the other end of the hallway.

"You're old, too," he yelled after me. "Take off that dress. You're revolting."

As I was going toward the door, I felt that I was precariously balanced on a sliver of the floor of the house of forty years before: it could still support my father, his easel, the bedroom, but I was afraid that my weight would cause it to collapse. I hurried out to the landing and shut the door carefully. Once in the open, I looked at the dress. Only then did I discover, with disgust, that at the level of the pubic area there was a large stain with a whitish edge. The material at that point was darker and, if you touched it, seemed starched.

22.

I went along the street. Around the corner I easily recognized the Coloniali, which had belonged to Caserta's father. It was shut up by two wooden boards crossed over a metal shutter that curled up on one side like the corner of the page of a book. Above, there was a mud-smeared sign on which one could make out: "Video Arcade." A cat with yellow eyes, the tail of a mouse wriggling in its mouth, emerged from the black triangle made by the broken shutter: it looked at me in alarm and then slipped cautiously out between the boards and the shutter and went off.

I kept going beside the wall of the building. I found the vents for the cellars. They were exactly as I remembered them: rectangular openings a foot or so from the pavement, each with nine bars across and covered by a fine screen. From them came cool air and a scent of dampness and dust. I looked inside, shading my eyes, trying to get used to the darkness. I saw nothing.

I went back to the entrance of the shop then, and observed the street. There was an untroubled clamor of children in a street that, with its poverty, was not reassuring at twilight. The hot air was saturated with a strong smell of gas, coming from the refineries. The water in the puddles was crowned with swarms of insects. On the sidewalk opposite children of four or five raced on plastic tricycles. A man of about fifty seemed to be wearily watching over them, his pants clinging to his belly under a bulging dirty yellow undershirt. He had massive arms, a long, hairy torso, short legs. He was leaning on the wall, next to an iron bar that didn't seem to belong to him: it was almost a meter long, sharpened at the tip—part of an old gate, left there by some boy who had recovered it from the garbage to play dangerous games. The man was smoking a cigar and staring at me.

I crossed the street and asked him, in dialect, if he could give me some matches. He took out of his pocket a box of kitchen matches and offered them to me, gazing ostentatiously at the stain on my dress. I took five, extracting them one by one, as if his look didn't embarrass me. He asked tonelessly if

I also wanted a cigar. I thanked him; I smoked neither cigars nor cigarettes. Then he told me that it was a mistake to go around alone. The place wasn't safe: there were some bad people who even bothered children. He pointed at them, grabbing the bar and giving it a rapid twist in their direction. They were insulting one another in dialect.

"Sons or grandsons?" I asked.

"Both," he answered peacefully. "I'll kill anyone who tries to touch them."

I thanked him again and went back across the street. I climbed over one of the boards, bent down, and entered the dark triangle beyond the shutter.

23.

I tried to orient myself as if the counter with the exotic scenes painted by my father so many years before were in front of me. I had felt it as huge, so high that it was at least two inches above my head. Then I realized that I had grown more than two feet since the time when I had lingered in front of that object loaded with licorice and sugared almonds. Immediately the wood and metal wall, which for a moment had been almost six feet high, slipped down and stopped at my hips. I walked around it cautiously. I even picked up my foot to climb onto the wooden platform behind the counter, but in vain: naturally, there was neither counter nor platform. I slid the soles of my shoes along the floor, groping my way, and encountered nothing, only debris and a few nails.

I decided to light a match. The place was empty and there existed no memory capable of filling it: only an overturned chair separated me from the opening that led into the space where Caserta's father had kept the machines for making sweets and ice cream. I let the match fall to keep from burning myself and went into the former *pasticceria*. There, though the right wall was blank, the left had three rectangular openings high up, barred and screened with mesh. There was enough light so that I could distinguish clearly a cot and, on it, a dark body, lying as if it were asleep. I cleared my throat to make myself heard but nothing happened. I lighted another match, approached, and reached out a hand toward the shadow lying on the bed. As I did so one hip bumped against a crate of the kind used to pack fruit. Something tumbled onto the floor, but the outline didn't move. I knelt down, with the flame grazing my fingertips. On all fours I hunted for the object I had heard falling. It was a metal flashlight. The match went out. With the beam of the flashlight I could discern a black plastic bag, left lying on the bed like a person sleeping. Some old underpants and an undershirt of Amalia's were strewn on the bare mattress.

"Are you here?" I asked in a hoarse voice, barely controlled.

There was no answer. So I rotated the beam of the flashlight. In one corner a rope had been stretched between the two walls. From it hung plastic hangers holding two shirts, a gray jacket and matching pants carefully folded, a raincoat. I examined the shirts: they had the same label as the one I had found in my mother's house. So I went on to search the pockets of the jacket, and there I found some change, seven telephone tokens, a second-class ticket from Naples to Rome via Formia, dated May 21st, three used bus tickets, two fruit candies, the receipt for a hotel in Formia, one bill for two single rooms, three receipts for three different bars, and the receipt for a restaurant in Minturno. The train ticket had been issued the same day my mother left Naples. The bill from the hotel, on the other hand, and the restaurant receipt, bore the date of the twenty-second. Caserta and Amalia's dinner had been lavish: two covers, 6,000 lire; two seafood antipasti, 30,000; two gnocchetti with shrimp, 20,000; two mixed fish grills, 40,000; two vegetables, 8,000; two ice creams, 12,000; two bottles of wine, 30,000.

A lot of food, wine. In general my mother ate very little, and a sip of wine made her head spin. I thought again of the phone calls she had made, of the obscenities she had spoken to me: maybe she wasn't frightened, maybe she was only happy; maybe she was happy and frightened. Amalia had the unpredictability of a splinter, I couldn't impose on her the prison of a single adjective. She had traveled with a man who had tormented her at least as much as her husband had and who continued subtly to torment her. With him she had left the line that went between Naples and Rome to slip sideways into a hotel room, a beach at night. She must not have been overly disturbed when Caserta's fetishism emerged more decisively. I felt her there, in the half-light, as if she were in that sack on the bed, constricted and curious, but not suffering. Certainly she had been pained by the discovery that that man was continuing to pursue her with perverse constancy, as he had done years before, when he had sent his gifts, knowing that he was exposing her to the brutality of her husband. I imagined her disoriented, when she found out that Caserta had gone to my father to talk about her, about the time they spent together. I saw that she was surprised that my father hadn't killed his presumed rival, as he had always threatened to do, but had listened to him calmly, in order then to spy on her, to beat her, to threaten her, to try to force his presence on her again. She had left in a great hurry, afraid, probably, of being followed by him. On the way, with Signora De Riso, she must have been certain of it. Once on the train she had sighed with relief and perhaps had expected Caserta to show up, to explain, to understand. I thought that she was confused and determined, anchored only to the suitcase in which she had the gifts for me. I roused myself and put back in Caserta's jacket pockets all those signs of their journey. In the bottom, in the seams, there was sand.

When I returned to my reconnaissance, I gasped. The beam of the flashlight, rotating, had passed by the silhouette of a woman standing against the wall opposite the bed. I brought the light back to the silhouette I had glimpsed. On a hanger attached to the wall was, in perfect order, the suit my mother had worn when she left: jacket and skirt of a material so durable that Amalia for decades had managed to adapt it, with slight modifications, to all the occasions that she considered important. Both garments were arranged on the hanger as if the person who had worn them had stepped out of them just for a moment, promising to return immediately. Under the jacket was an old blue shirt, very familiar to me. Hesitantly I stuck one hand under the collar and found one of Amalia's ancient bras attached with a diaper pin to the shirt. I felt inside the skirt: there were her mended underpants. On the floor I saw the worn and unfashionable low-heeled shoes, many times resoled, that had belonged to her, and the stockings that lay over them like a veil.

I sat on the edge of the bed. I had to try to keep the suit from detaching itself from the wall. I wanted each of those garments to stay put, motionless, and use up the rest of the energy that Amalia had left there. I let each stitch become unsewed, the blue material become again the uncut fabric, smelling like new, not even touched by Amalia, who, a young girl in a red-and-blue flowered American dress, was still choosing among the bolts of material, in a shop that smelled intensely of fabric. She discussed happily. She was still planning to sew it herself, she was still touching the selvage, she was lifting an edge to calculate the bias. But I wasn't able to contain her for long. Amalia was already working eagerly. She spread over the material the paper that reproduced the parts of her body. She attached it with pins, piece to piece. She cut it, holding the fabric with the thumb and middle finger of her left hand. She basted. She was sparing with her stitches. She measured, she

took out stitches, she restitched. She lined. Oh, I was fascinated by her art of constructing a double. I saw the dress growing
like another body, a more accessible body. How many times
had I sneaked into the armoire in the bedroom, closed the
door, sat in the dark among her clothes, under the redolent
skirt of that suit, breathing in her body, clothing myself in it? I
was enthralled by her ability to extract a person from the woof
and warp of the fabric, a mask that was nourished on warmth
and scent, which seemed character, theater, story. Even if she
had never let me touch it, that silhouette of hers had certainly
been, up to the threshold of my adolescence, generous with
suggestions, images, pleasures. The suit was alive.

Caserta, too, must have thought so. On that dress his body
had surely lain, when in the course of the last year a senile
understanding had grown up between them, which I had failed
to value in all its intensity and all its implications. In that dress
she had left in a hurry, agitated after my father's revelations,
suspicious, fearful of being watched still. In that dress Amalia's
body had touched Caserta, when he sat down beside her suddenly, in the train. Had they arranged to meet? Now I saw
them together, as they met in the compartment, just outside the
view of Signora De Riso. Amalia still graceful, slender, with
that old-fashioned hair; him tall, lean, neat: a handsome old
couple. But perhaps there was no agreement between them:
Caserta had followed her onto the train on his own initiative,
had sat down beside her, had begun to talk to her, appealing,
as it appeared he was able to be. Yet, however things had gone,
I doubted that Amalia intended to arrive at my house with
him: maybe Caserta had merely offered to keep her company
during the journey, maybe on the way she had begun to tell
him about our summer vacations, maybe, as had happened to
her in recent months, she had begun to lose her sense of things,
to forget my father, to forget that the man sitting beside her
was obsessed with her, with her person, her body, her way of

being, but also with a revenge that was more and more abstract, less and less concrete, pure fantasy among the many fantasies of old age.

Or no: she still had him in mind and was already planning, as she did with clothes, the turn she would give to the last events of her existence. Anyway, the destination had suddenly changed, not by the will of Caserta. Surely it had been Amalia who urged him to get out at Formia. He could have had no interest in returning to the places where we (my father, her, me, my sisters) had gone swimming in the fifties. It was possible, however, that Amalia, convinced that my father, hiding somewhere, had persisted in secretly spying on them, had decided to lead that spy on a journey that might petrify him.

They had eaten in cafés, had drunk: certainly a new game had begun, which Amalia had not foreseen but which had seduced her. The first telephone call she had made to me bore witness to a confusion that excited her and at the same time disoriented her. And although they had taken separate rooms in the hotel, the second phone call made me doubt that Amalia had been locked in her room. In that old outfit for important occasions I felt the force that was pushing her out of the house, away from me, and the risk that she would never return. I saw in the blue fabric the dark night of the storeroom next to her bedroom, where I shut myself up to fight with terror the terror of losing her forever. No, Amalia had not stayed in her room.

The next day, they had arrived together in Minturno, probably on the train, maybe by bus. In the evening they had had dinner heedless of the expense, gaily, even ordering two bottles of wine. Then they had walked on the beach at night. I knew that, on the beach, my mother had put on the clothes that she had earlier intended to give me. Maybe it was Caserta who had induced her to undress and put on the clothes, the lingerie, the bathrobe that he had stolen for her from the Vossi sisters' shop. Maybe Amalia had done it spontaneously, made uninhibited by the wine, obsessed by the neurotic vigilance of her former husband. Violence could be ruled out: violence that the autopsy would have verified had not been verified.

I saw her step out of her old suit, and I had the impression that it stood stiff and desolate, suspended over the cold sand as it was suspended now against the wall. I saw her staggering, drunk, as she tried to put on that luxurious lingerie, garments too youthful. I saw her until, exhausted, she had wrapped herself in the satin dressing gown. She must have seen that something had in a sense slipped away forever: with my father, with Caserta, maybe even with me, when she had decided to change her itinerary. She herself had slipped away: the telephone calls she had made to me, probably in the company of Caserta, were, with their happy desperation, perhaps meant to indicate only the confusion of the situation she found herself in, the disorientation she was experiencing. Certainly when she had gone naked into the water, she had done it by choice. I felt that she imagined herself caught between two sets of pupils, expropriated by two gazes. And I felt her discover, worn out, that my father wasn't there, that Caserta was pursuing the fantasies of a witless old man—that the spectators of that scene were absent. She had abandoned the satin bathrobe, she had kept on only the Vossi bra. Probably Caserta was there, looking without seeing. But I wasn't sure. Maybe he had already gone off with Amalia's clothes. Or maybe she herself had ordered him to go. I doubted that he had taken away dresses and lingerie on his own. But I was certain that Amalia had insisted that he deliver the gifts to me, and that he had promised he would: a final exchange, in order to obtain the old lingerie that was dear to him. They must have talked about me, of what I had done as a little child. Or maybe I had long ago entered into the small-time sadistic game that Caserta was leading. Certainly I was a part of his senile fantasies, and he wanted to take revenge on me as if I were the child of forty years earlier. I imagined

Caserta on the sand, stunned by the sound of the tide and by the dampness, as disoriented as Amalia, drunk as she was, and incapable of understanding how far the game had gone. I was afraid he hadn't even realized that the mouse with which he had amused himself for a good part of his life was fleeing, to go and drown herself.

24.

I got up from the bed mainly so that I would no longer see the blue silhouette hanging on the opposite wall. I could make out the steps that led to the door to the building's courtyard. There were five, I remembered clearly: I used to play with Antonio, jumping up and down them while his grandfather was making pastries. I counted them as I went up. Arriving at the top, I realized with surprise that the door wasn't locked but pulled to; the lock was broken. Evidently the old man came and went that way. I opened it and looked out: on one side was the doorway that opened to the courtyard, on the other the flight of stairs going up to what had once upon a time been Caserta's apartment. Filippo and my father had followed him up those stairs to murder him. At first he had tried to fight back; then he had stopped.

I looked up from the bottom of the stairs, and my neck ached. I had a view decades old that wanted to show me more than I could now see. The story, shattered into a thousand incoherent images, struggled to correspond to stone and iron. But the violence came to an end now, wrapped around the railing of the stairway, and it seemed to me that it had been here—here and not there—for forty years, screaming. Caserta had stopped fighting not for lack of strength or admission of guilt or cowardice but because Uncle Filippo, on the fifth floor, had grabbed Antonio and—yes, that was it—dangled him by the ankles, cursing in a hostile dialect, the language of my mother. My uncle was young, and had both his arms, and threatened to drop the child if Caserta made so much as a hint of a movement. My father's work was easy.

Leaving the door open I went back into the cellar. With the flashlight I looked for the little door that led to the lower level. I remembered that it was iron, and painted, perhaps brown. I found a wooden door, no more than a foot and a half high: a window more than a door, half closed, with a little hole in the panel and one in the frame: an open padlock was hanging in the latter.

Seeing it I had to admit immediately that the image of Caserta and Amalia going in and out through that door upright and radiant, at times arm in arm, at times holding hands, she in her suit, he in the camelhair coat, was a lie of memory. Even Antonio and I had to bend down to get through. Childhood is a tissue of lies that endure in the past tense: at least, mine was like that. But I heard the cries of the children in the street and it seemed to me that they were not dissimilar from the way I had been: they shouted in the same dialect; each imagined something else. They were invention, while they spent the evening on the dirty sidewalk under the eye of the man in the undershirt. They rushed around on tricycles and yelled insults punctuated by piercing cries of joy. Insults with a sexual basis: at times into their obscene jargon the voice of the man with the iron bar inserted even harsher obscenities.

I let out a faint groan. I heard myself repeating to Antonio words no different from those I was listening to, behind that door, in the black subterranean space; and he repeated them to me. But I was lying when I said them. I was pretending not to be me. I didn't want to be "I," unless it was the I of Amalia. I did what I imagined Amalia did in secret. And, lacking journeys of hers that I could be part of, I imposed on her my journeys from home to the Coloniali, the shop of the old man Caserta. She left the house, turned the corner, pushed open the glass door, tasted creams, waited for her playmate. I was I and I was her. I-her met each other with Caserta. In fact I saw not the face of Antonio, when Antonio appeared in the doorway from the courtyard, but what there was in his face of the adult face of his father.

I loved Caserta with the intensity with which I imagined my mother loved him. And I loathed him, because the fantasy of that secret love was so vivid and concrete that I felt I could never be loved in the same way: not by him but by her, Amalia. Caserta had taken what was rightfully mine. As I moved around the painted counter, I moved like her, I talked to myself re-creating her voice, I batted my eyelashes, I laughed the way my father didn't want her to laugh. Then I went up on the wooden platform and entered the *pasticceria* with the movements of a woman. Antonio's grandfather was squeezing out waves of cream from the cloth bag and he looked at me with deep-set eyes, veiled by the heat of the ovens.

I pulled open the little door and shone the beam of the flashlight inside. I squatted down, knees against my chest, head tilted. Bent over like this, I slid down three slippery steps. I agreed, on the way, to tell myself everything: whatever truth the lies preserved.

I was surely Amalia when, one day, I found the *pasticceria* empty and the little door open. I was Amalia, who, naked as the Gypsy painted by my father, around whom insults, oaths, threats had been flying for weeks, slipped into the dark cellar with Caserta. I was, in the past tense. I felt I was her, with her thoughts, free and happy, having escaped from the sewing machine, the gloves, the needle and thread, my father, his paintings, the yellow paper on which she ended up in blood-red scrawls. I was identical to her and yet I suffered because of the incompleteness of that identity. We succeeded in being "I" only in the game now, and I knew it.

But Caserta, stooping at the bottom of the three steps beyond the door, looked at me obliquely and said, "Come."

While I invented his voice giving sound to "Amalia," along with the verb, he ran a knotty finger, dirty with cream, lightly up one leg, under the dress my mother had sewed for me. At that touch I felt pleasure. And I realized that the obscene things that the man was mumbling hoarsely, as he touched me, were happening in detail in my head. I memorized them and it seemed to me that he said them with a long red tongue that spoke not from his mouth but from his pants. I was breathless. I felt pleasure and fear at the same time. I tried to contain both, but I realized resentfully that the game wasn't going well. It was Amalia who felt all the pleasure: only fear was left for me. The more things happened, the more irritated I became, because I couldn't be "I" in her pleasure, and I could only shudder.

Besides, even Caserta wasn't convincing. Sometimes he managed to be Caserta, sometimes his features faded. This alarmed me more and more. It was happening the way it did with Antonio: during our games, I was Amalia with conviction, he was his father fleetingly, maybe for lack of imagination. I hated him then. If he was Antonio, then I was merely Delia, down in the cellar, with one hand on his sex; and meanwhile, somewhere, Amalia was playing at being really Amalia, excluding me from her game just as the girls in the courtyard sometimes did.

So at a certain point I had to give in and admit that the man who said to me "Come" at the bottom of the three cellar steps was the seller of *coloniali*, the dark old man who made ice cream and sweets, the grandfather of little Antonio, the father of Caserta. But Caserta no: Caserta was certainly somewhere else, with my mother. So I pushed him off and ran away crying. I jumped onto the fragment of floor where my father was, the easel, the bedroom. I reported to him, in the coarse dialect of the courtyard, the obscene things that man had done and said to me. I wept. I had clear in my mind the old man's face disfigured by the flush of his skin and by fear.

Caserta, I said to my father. I said to him that Caserta had done and said to Amalia, with her consent, in the basement of the pastry shop, all the things that in reality Antonio's grandfather had said and perhaps done to me. He stopped working and waited for my mother to return home.

To speak is to link together lost times and spaces. I sat on the top step, believing it was the same step as then. One by one, I whispered to myself the obscene formulas that Caserta's father had repeated with growing agitation forty years earlier. And I realized that, in substance, they were the same that my mother had cried to me, giggling, over the telephone, before going to drown herself. Words for being lost or for being found. Maybe she wanted to communicate to me that she, too, hated me for what I had done to her forty years earlier. Maybe in that way she wished to make me understand who the man was who was there with her. Maybe she wanted to tell me to watch out for myself, to beware of Caserta's senile ravings. Or maybe she simply wanted to show me that those words, too, could be uttered, and that, contrary to what I had believed my whole life, they couldn't hurt me.

I seized on that last hypothesis. I was there, curled up on the threshold of tormented fantasies, to see Caserta and tell him that I had never wanted to hurt him. The story between him and my mother no longer interested me: I wished only to confess aloud that, then and later, I had hated not him, perhaps not even his father: only Amalia. It was she I wanted to hurt. Because she had left me in the world to play alone with the words of a lie, without limits, without truth.

25.

But Caserta didn't appear. In the basement there were only empty cardboard boxes and old carbonated water or beer bot-

tles. I crawled out, dusty, irritated by the light touch of spider-
webs, and returned to the cot. On the floor I saw my blood-
stained underpants and kicked them under the bed with the
toe of my shoe. Now it bothered me more to find them in that
place, like a purloined part of myself, than to imagine the use
that Caserta had made of them.

I went back to the wall where Amalia's blue suit was hanging. I took down the hanger, I laid the garment delicately on
the bed, I removed the jacket: the lining was threadbare, the
pockets were empty. I held it against me as if I wanted to see
how it looked. Then I made up my mind: I put the flashlight
down on the cot, I took off my dress and left it on the floor;
then I dressed again, carefully, without haste. I used the safety
pin that Caserta had used to attach the bra to the shirt to take
in the waist: it was too big. The jacket, too, was large and yet I
arranged it to my satisfaction. I felt that that old garment was
the final narrative that my mother had left me, and that now,
with all the necessary adjustments, it fit me like a glove.

The story might be more fragile or more interesting than
the one I had told myself. It was enough to pull out a single
thread and follow it in its simplifying linearity. For example,
Amalia had left with her old lover and with him had spent a
final secret vacation, laughing loudly, eating and drinking,
stripping on the beach, putting on and taking off the clothes
that she intended to give me. The game of an old woman pretending to be young, to please another old person. Finally, she
had decided to go swimming naked. But, bright as it was, she
had gone too far from the shore and had drowned. Caserta had
been afraid, had picked up everything and left. Or she was
running naked along the water's edge and he was following,
both of them panting, both terrified, she by the discovery of
his desires, he by her rejection. Until Amalia thought that she
could escape into the water.

Yes, it was enough to pull one thread to go on playing with

the mysterious figure of my mother, now enriching it, now humiliating it. But I realized that I no longer felt the need, and I moved in the ray of light just as it seemed to me that she had moved. I turned off the flashlight and leaned toward the bluish triangle of the shutter to stick my head out. The streetlamps were on, but there was still light. The children were no longer running and shouting. They were gathered around a man who was crouching, his face at the height of their faces, his hands on his knees. The man was Caserta. He had thick white hair and an engaging look. They were all standing, the little ones, the big one, with their shoes in a puddle that shone in the light. The children had begun to unwrap the candies that he had just handed out.

I looked at that lean old man, carefully shaved, well dressed, his face pale and tense, and I no longer felt the need to speak to him, to know, to let him know. I decided to steal away along the sidewalk, around the corner, but he turned and saw me. His astonishment was such that he didn't realize what was happening behind him. The man in the undershirt had leaned the bar against the wall carefully, had thrown away his cigar, and now was approaching, looking straight ahead, chest erect, short legs taking rational, calm steps. The children backed away, retreating from the puddle. Caserta remained alone in the mirror of the violet water, mouth open, eyes staring at me without anxiety. That tranquility helped me breathe. I went back into the Coloniali of forty years earlier, I was careful not to bump into the counter with its palm trees and camels, I climbed onto the wooden platform, crossed the *pasticceria,* expertly skirting the oven, the machines, the counters, the pans, went out the door that opened onto the courtyard. Once in the open I searched for the proper pace of a grownup person who is not in a hurry.

26.

The gas burned in the night on the tops of the refineries. I was traveling on a local train slow as a death, having looked for and found a lighted compartment, without sleeping passengers. I wanted if not the entire train at least my seat to maintain its solidity. I found a place with some boys in their twenties, recruits returning from a short leave. Speaking an almost incomprehensible dialect, they displayed in every phrase a frightened aggressiveness. They had missed the train that would have got them to the barracks on time. They knew they would be punished and were afraid. But they wouldn't confess it. Instead, with shouts and sneers, they imagined subjecting the officers who would punish them to sexual humiliations of every type. They placed these in an indeterminate future and, in the meantime, described them exhaustively. They declared, addressing me, but obliquely, that they weren't afraid of anyone. Every time, their glances became bolder. One of them began to speak to me directly and offered me beer from the can he had been drinking from. I drank some. The others, their bodies contracted by stifled laughter, pressed together, and then, turning purple, pushed each other away.

I left them at Minturno. I walked to the Appian highway, through deserted streets, among empty ordinary bungalows. It was still dark when I succeeded in finding the house of our holidays, a two-story structure with a sloping roof, locked up and silent in the dew. As soon as it was light I set off on a sandy path, populated only by beetles and motionless lizards, waiting for the early warmth. The reeds with which I had made kite frames for my sisters and me wet the suit as I grazed them.

I took off my shoes and sank my aching feet into the fine sand, which was cold and dirty, strewn with debris of every sort. I sat on the trunk of a tree near the shore, waiting for the sun to warm me, but also to attach my presence to some object solidly rooted in the sand. The sea now was calm and blue under the sun, but the rays came just to the water's edge, leaving the sand in a gray shadow. A thin mist that would soon evaporate was still hiding the stubble fields, the hills, the mountains. I had already returned to that place, after my mother's death. I had seen neither the sea nor the beach. I had seen only details: the white shell of a conch, with its regular striations; a crab with sections of its abdomen turned to the sun, the green plastic of a detergent bottle; that trunk I was sitting on. I had asked myself why my mother had decided to die in that place. I would never know. I was the only possible source of the story: I couldn't nor did I want to search outside myself.

When the sun began to touch me, I heard Amalia, who was young and full of amazement at the appearance of the first bikinis. She said: "You could hold both pieces in one hand." She, however, wore a green costume that she had made herself, high-necked, sturdy, intended to suffocate shapes, and over the years it remained the same. Prudently she often checked to be sure that the fabric wasn't riding up on her thighs or her buttocks. On Sundays, apparently by choice, she would be wrapped in a towel as if she were cold, on a beach chair under the umbrella, beside my father. But she wasn't cold. On holidays groups of curly-haired boys arrived at the beach, from inland, in indecent bathing suits, faces, necks, and arms burned by the sun, white everywhere else, noisy, quarrelsome, fighting furiously on the sand or in the water, sometimes in fun, sometimes seriously. My father, who generally spent the time at the water's edge, eating clams dug out of the sand, when he saw them changed mood and attitude. He ordered Amalia not to leave the umbrella. He watched her to see if she glanced at them out of the corners of her eyes. When the boys came too close to the umbrella in the course of their games, laughing, and sandy up to their hair, he quickly joined us and compelled us all four to stay near him. Meanwhile with fierce looks he declared war on the youths. We, as always, were afraid.

But what I remembered with greater dismay about those holidays was the outdoor movies, where we went often. My father, to protect us from possible annoyance, made the youngest of my sisters sit in the first seat in the row, the one on the center aisle. Then he ordered the next to sit beside her. I followed, then my mother, finally him. Amalia had an expression between amused and admiring. But I interpreted that arrangement of seats as a sign of danger and became more and more anxious. When my father sat in his place and put an arm around the shoulders of his wife, the gesture seemed to me the ultimate fortification against an obscure threat that would soon be revealed.

The film would begin but I felt that he was not calm. He watched nervously. If by chance Amalia turned to look behind her he immediately did so, too. At regular intervals he asked her: "What's wrong?" She reassured him but my father didn't trust her. I was influenced by his anxiety. I thought that if something happened to me—something terrible, I didn't know what—I would be silent about it. I deduced, I don't know why, that Amalia would behave the same way. But this knowledge made me even more fearful. Because, if my father had discovered that she had hidden from him the attempt of some stranger to approach, he would immediately have the proof of all Amalia's other innumerable assents.

I already had those proofs. When we went to the movies without him, my mother didn't respect any of the rules that he imposed: she looked around freely, she laughed as she wasn't supposed to laugh, and chatted with people she didn't know, for example with the candy seller, who when the lights went out and the starry sky appeared sat down next to her. So when my father was there I couldn't follow the story of the film. I glanced around furtively in the darkness to exercise, in my turn, control over Amalia, to anticipate the discovery of her secrets, to keep him, too, from discovering her guilt. Amid the smoke of cigarettes and the glow from the band of light emitted by the projector, I fearfully imagined bodies of men in the shape of frogs who jumped agilely under the rows of seats, extending not paws but hands and sticky tongues. So in spite of the heat I was covered with an icy sweat.

But when her husband was there Amalia, after a stealthy look sideways, curious and yet apprehensive, let her head fall on my father's shoulder and appeared happy. That double movement tortured me. I didn't know where to follow my mother in flight, if along the axis of that glance or along the parabola that her hair made in the direction of her husband's shoulder. I was beside her, trembling. Even the stars, so thick in summer, seemed to me points of my confusion. I was to such an extent determined to become different from her that, one by one, I lost the reasons for resembling her.

The sun began to warm me. I dug in my purse and took out my identification card. I stared for a long time at the photograph, studying myself in search of Amalia in that image. It was a recent photo, taken when I renewed the document. With a pen, as the sun burned my neck, I drew around my own features my mother's hair. I lengthened the short hair, moving from the ears and making two broad bands that met in a black wave, over the forehead. I sketched a rebel curl over the right eye, barely contained between the hairline and the eyebrow. I looked at myself, smiled at myself. That old-fashioned hairstyle, popular in the forties but already rare at the end of the fifties, suited me. Amalia had been. I was Amalia.

About the Author

Elena Ferrante is the author of *The Days of Abandonment* (Europa, 2005), *Troubling Love* (Europa, 2006), and *The Lost Daughter* (Europa, 2008), now a film directed by Maggie Gyllenhaal and starring Olivia Colman, Dakota Johnson, and Paul Mescal. She is also the author of *Incidental Inventions* (Europa, 2019), illustrated by Andrea Ucini, *Frantumaglia: A Writer's Journey* (Europa, 2016), *In the Margins: On the Pleasures of Reading and Writing* (Europa, 2022), and *The Beach at Night* (Europa, 2016), a children's picture book illustrated by Mara Cerri. The four volumes known as the "Neapolitan quartet" (*My Brilliant Friend, The Story of a New Name, Those Who Leave and Those Who Stay,* and *The Story of the Lost Child*) were published by Europa Editions between 2012 and 2015. *My Brilliant Friend,* the HBO series directed by Saverio Costanzo, premiered in 2018. The adaptation of Ferrante's most recent novel, *The Lying Life of Adults* (Europa, 2020), debuted on Netflix in 2023.